REAL COLD

WEB OF LIES
BOOK THREE

KATY LEE

CHAPTER 1

*V*era Sharp approached the target. Her black sequined cocktail dress shimmered in the chandelier light with each clicking step of her stilettos. Across the dance floor, Nico Rossi, the notorious mobster, sat at a table talking with his associate, or more like mumbling. She needed to get closer to hear what they spoke about, as his lips were unreadable.

A man stepped in her path. "Care to dance, beautiful?"

Vera's eyes never left Nico's face. Her hand brushed the man away as she sidestepped him.

"I see who you're after." The man slipped into the crowd with a chuckle. "You're playing with fire."

The last of his words trickled to her ear as a

woman to her right threw her head back and laughed at something her date whispered to her. The man didn't know that playing with fire was part of Vera's job.

A server cut in front of her with a tray of filled champagne flutes. "For the toast," the woman said and passed her a glass.

Vera took an obligatory glass, carrying it with her to Nico's table. She glanced at the golden liquid and smiled to herself, noticing the stillness of the drink. Most people would shake in their boots, approaching the infamous New York crime lord without an invitation.

But not her…because he had given her one.

She had never been this close to him, but this was the moment that all the blood, sweat and tears of her FBI training had prepared her for. There was nothing that could stop her from taking him down. First, she had impressed him with her singing on the stage. She'd made sure she chose his favorite tunes, learning all about his late wife's foray into her own stage life and how they met fifty years ago.

Vera stepped up to the table, using the stem of the flute to hide the minuscule black dot recorder she held in her palm. She stood off to his left shoulder and lightly cleared her throat.

Rossi stopped talking abruptly and turned her way. A slow smile crept over his aging face. His entire dark demeanor was the epitome of a mafia godfather, right down to the wave of his pointer finger toward his associate.

"Leave us," he said under his breath, and the man disappeared into the crowd. Though, Vera knew the man most likely didn't go far. A collection of Rossi's bodyguards also stood nearby, their hands clasped in front of them as they surveyed the crowd stoically for an intruder, an enemy.

They watched her beneath their lids, not knowing they were staring at one.

Placing the bug on him would have to be smooth and fast. But that was what she was known for in the Bureau.

"You asked to see me?" Vera pretended to be nervous, slightly averting her gaze from the mob man.

"Dance with me." Nico Rossi pushed back from the table and offered her a hand, taking her glass from her to place on the table.

Vera quickly gave him her other hand instead, keeping the device safe in her palm. A tango across the dance floor would be the perfect time to place the listening chip into his coat pocket. Her intel had informed her the meeting would go down tonight. With the recorder in place, she would be sure to hear everything about his next heist. Even if she only heard a few hours of conversation, it could be enough to direct her next steps in the case.

As he led her across the floor, she thought of the images of his last illegal enterprise. The blood of an innocent woman spilled across the bank's marble floor. She mentally closed the brief in her mind to focus on the despicable man taking her into his arms. Before she could slip her hand into his pocket, he spun her off to his side, bringing her back, so she faced away from him. His hot breath brushed the side of her neck as he held her in place.

"You sing like a bird," he whispered, and her stomach churned. "You dance like you're floating on a cloud. Is there anything you can't do on stage?"

"Do you mean act?" Vera turned her head to the side to coyly catch his eye, thinking of her life as an undercover agent. Acting *was* her life. "Yes, I can do all three."

"My wife was a triple threat, too. You remind me of her."

That was the point. Vera held her breath to find out if her plan worked.

Or would Nico take her out back and make her

disappear for having the gall to make him remember his wife? Before she could read him, he swung her back out, this time bringing her back to face him at an abrupt stop.

Vera clung to the device in her palm, but she couldn't hold on to it much longer. Her scalp under the wig itched, and she did her best to ignore the creeping prickle. Rossi liked his women, tall and dark-haired, and the bigger the hair, the better. For the mission, she covered her blond strands with full, dark red waves.

"You are stunning." The smell of cognac and cigars wafted from his lips.

Vera swallowed a cringe and leaned in, just barely brushing her lips to his. "Thank you," she whispered in her low, singing voice. He released her hand and cupped her cheek as she placed her other hand at his waist, slipping the device into the pocket at the same time.

Done.

Now, all she had left to do was wait for the meeting later. She would join her handler in the surveillance van two streets over and listen with glee as Rossi incriminated himself. Agent Mark Tangen once compared her to a cheetah, and it was time for her to swiftly slip out the back.

Vera backed away from the kiss Rossi was about to plant on her lips. She took control of the dance and led him with her cheek pressed against his for the last portion of the tango. Before he could dip her, she stepped from his embrace.

"You're a good dancer yourself, Mr. Rossi." She'd read in his file that he loved flattery. "Thank you for the invitation tonight. I'm humbled that you enjoyed the show."

"Leaving so soon?" He took a step closer. "And please, you're to call me Nico."

Vera bit her lower lip and dropped her gaze. "I mean, I didn't want to assume...or intrude."

"Nonsense." He gripped her wrist, displaying his strength a little too tightly. He purred as he said, "You'll be my guest the rest of this evening, Miss Moon. Or may I call you Roxie? It's only fair."

Roxie Moon was her undercover name, meant to infiltrate shady establishments from the backstage door. She'd opted not to wear a wire that night, against Tangen's warnings. She knew once she stepped away from Rossi and his bug, she would be going alone. Did Nico sense something was up?

No time to find out. It was time for her to run.

"Absolutely," she purred right back. "Just give me

a few moments to go to the ladies' room, and then I'm all yours."

He brushed her cheek, flashing a large gold ring on his finger. It was sharp and could do some damage with one blow. "Good. I have a quick meeting, so make yourself comfortable at the table, and I'll be back shortly. Order anything you want."

Vera slipped from his hand, careful to hide any tension in her limbs from the excitement about what she would hear in that meeting. A quick glance to her right showed the direction of the restrooms. She took two steps before his hand gripped her again. This time her forearm and much harder.

"Have we met before? I never forget a face, and when you turned, you reminded me of someone."

Vera laughed, shaking her head. "I'm sure I would've remembered such an event. Perhaps you've seen me perform before tonight?" She held her voice in check, staying in character. "Carnegie? Rockefeller?"

Nico tilted his head. His black eyes turned onyx. His jawline feathered where he clenched it. A small scar popped out on his upper right cheek from the days when he did his own fighting...killing. "Maybe."

Vera cracked a light smile and leaned close.

"Whether or not we've met before, after tonight, we'll know each other a whole lot better."

It wasn't a lie, but she held her breath until Nico's hard-lined face relaxed and he let out a deep laugh of his own. "Hurry back, sweet Roxie."

She pressed a kiss to the tips of her fingers and touched his mouth. "You, too."

Vera made her way toward the bathrooms, at first in slow speed, then picking up when she turned the corner out of Nico's sight. Tangen was probably screaming his head off right now. She could picture her handler and the lecture she would receive when she reached the van. The mission had been a success but barely. Things could have gone south fast. And still could.

Roxie Moon reached the bathroom, and glancing over her shoulder, she bypassed the door. She was sure Nico would have one of his goons watching for her to come out. Only Roxie would not be exiting the bathroom.

Slipping down the next corridor, Vera slunk up to a door beneath the hallway's camera, out of sight of the footage, and entered. The light from the hall shined on extra chairs and tables that lined the walls. It would be her makeshift changing room. She closed the door, letting the crack of light beneath it be her only guide. She found the bag she had stashed there earlier and made haste. The wig came off first, then the dress and heels. Big, round glasses covered half her face. Thirty seconds later, she peeked out the door to find the hall empty, stepping out dressed now as a server in a black uniform.

More black.

Vera hated the color black. It washed out her pale complexion. But as she exited the closet, Roxie Moon was nowhere in sight, and that was all that mattered.

Vera touched her head to smooth her flyaway hair and realized the wig netting still clung to her bun. She snatched it quickly, just as someone called from behind, their deep voice swinging her about.

"Where do you think you're going?" The maître d' drilled piercing eyes her way.

Vera touched her stomach. "Something I ate, sir. I need to go outside for a little while to get some air."

"You leave this building, and you are fired. You understand me? Give me your name badge."

Vera covered her mouth and choked back her best gag as she pivoted. She shook her head as she took off running, her backpack of Roxie's belongings swinging behind her.

Vera gave Nico about twenty minutes before he

realized he had been stood up. A search would ensue. But as far as anyone was concerned, the only person who left the building was a sick, unnamed employee. Roxie Moon had just disappeared.

Vera looked forward to hearing the foul mood Nico would be in when she was safely in the surveillance van. That meeting he mentioned was going off right at this moment. By the time she reached the van, she hoped she would have her next orders.

Just wait until he found out she was FBI.

Vera walked out onto the snowy streets of Manhattan and merged at the crosswalk with the holiday crowd excited about Christmas in four weeks. She knew her path would soon cross Nico Rossi's again. She hoped she would be the one to cuff him. Each cinch cutting into his skin to make up for all the pain he caused his victims, including her family.

The truth was, they had met before...the day he killed her parents.

"You're fired. Now get out of my restaurant."

Rafe Sinclair stepped out of the kitchen's swinging doors to hear his restaurant manager firing another employee. The young woman barely stifled a laugh in Gus's face.

"Fine with me. I can't make tips if there are no customers. See ya." She burst out the glass door, disappearing down the sloshy city street.

Rafe leaned against the host counter, crossing his arms. "*Your* restaurant? What was wrong with that one?"

"She was late three times this week. And you heard her. She wasn't happy here, anyway. And it showed. I say, good riddance." Gus Vargas watched Carrie or Carlie or whatever her name was through the glass before he returned to the host station, shrugging the incident off as he flicked a nonexistent speck from his dark brown suit coat.

Rafe lifted his head and waved at the empty restaurant. Tables and chairs draped in white linen and fine china stood ready for the customers who'd stopped showing up months ago. "Late for what? No one is here, and no one is coming. Christmas is in three weeks. This place should be hopping. And that was the third server in less than a month. We really need to stop hiring pretty girls nearly half our age."

"This is New York City. The servers are the first faces customers see before they taste your food."

"If only I could tease the people walking down the streets with samples of the cuisine. They would see Creare lived up to all Mel Mesini dreamed the place would be. Creare means to create in Italian, and I have always made creating the most delectable menu my focus. One bite of my *osso buco Milanese* would have them pushing every other customer to the floor for the best seats in Creare. I don't understand where all the customers went. This place used to be packed every night. I don't know how to get them back. I know New York restaurants rise and fall, but I never thought I would see Creare fall so easily and so fast."

Gus was his manager, but more importantly, he was Rafe's oldest friend. He'd known him since he was fifteen years old. He stepped up to the plate to help him stay above water after Mel and Chris, Rafe's two business partners, moved away to get married. He patted Rafe on the back.

"Business will pick up. And believe it or not, the books aren't that bad. I changed your suppliers who were robbing you blind, saving you tons. You've got a good two months before you have to close the doors for good. Have you thought about changing the menu?"

"My menu is fine. It's the changes out here in the dining room that are needed. This was Christina and Mel's expertise. They knew how to bring the crowds in. I just know how to cook."

Gus sniffed a laugh. "Didn't Mel get the place shut down with bad publicity?"

Rafe bit back a smile. "Yeah, she did. But it wasn't her fault some mentally deranged man stalked her. And you know there's no such thing as bad publicity. Creare had its best sales after Mel was nearly killed. People came from all over to dine here."

"Because of your cooking."

"Sure. I can say I had a big part in it. Christina also knew how to find the best stage talent to keep the place booming. I just don't have the knowledge to audition people." Rafe glanced at the stage that now had a large round table on it for a private party. "I wanted to upscale to fine dining. Maybe I was wrong."

Gus walked to the stage, large enough for a small band. A large window behind it looked out onto a winter cityscape. "I don't think celebrity tactics will keep the customers coming back. Let your flaming crème brûlée do that. And you don't need some wannabe singer to keep the doors open, either."

"Then what do you suggest, Gumbo?" It was the nickname from their time at the Culinary Arts Institute. Rafe went for cooking, while Gus studied hospitality. His family was in the hotel business, among other customer-related enterprises. They were successful, so they must be doing something right. "I hired you to bring this place back to life, but it's more dead now than ever."

"Do you want to take over the hiring?" Gus raised his hands, looking offended.

Rafe bit back the accusatory words on his tongue. It was easy to lay blame on someone else, but that wouldn't help him right now. And it wouldn't be fair. Plus, Gus was the only friend who had ever stood by him through whatever life threw at him. He was the only person Rafe could be sure would take a bullet for him...not that Rafe ever expected to be shot at.

"No. Not a chance. I trust you with the waitstaff, but is there money available to hire someone?"

"Maybe a couple of servers. Let me ask my family. One of my uncles might recommend someone from their hotels."

Rafe smiled, feeling hopeful that things could be

turned around for the better. "Remember, I don't want to owe anyone anything."

"I know."

Becoming an owner of Creare had been a dream come true. To lose it now would make Rafe feel like a failure. If Creare closed its doors, he would have to be honest that it was he who ran it into the ground and no one else.

He hit the swinging doors into his kitchen. "And no more pretty girls! I mean that. Got it, Gumbo?"

Gus sputtered, clutching his chest. "Who are you, and what have you done with Rafe?"

Rafe ignored the comment about his history with women and called back, "Oh, and just to be clear. It's *my* restaurant."

The swinging doors had the last word and closed on Gus.

Rafe entered the kitchen, wanting to focus solely on what he excelled at and the only thing he could believe in. Food never let him down. Cooking saved him from a life on the streets. When everyone else went AWOL, his next dish and chef's knife stuck by his side.

He moved to the first station where his pantry chef prepped the night's salads and appetizers. Rafe wondered how much of the food would go to waste that night. He patted Monroe on the back as he passed by.

"Always so colorful," Rafe said, referencing the explosion of color in the mixing bowl. He recently let his sous chef go, so Monroe filled both roles, as well as the role of dishwasher. Once he was gone, Rafe would be handling everything.

Who was he kidding?

When Monroe was gone, they would all be done. Creare would exist no more.

Rafe ran his fingers through his black curls and placed his white chef's toque on his head. He reached for his favorite knife with a porcelain hilt and sliced into the tenderloin.

Too tough.

Fighting the desire to throw the knife across the room, he brought it down on the stainless steel countertop and took three deep breaths. Then he bellowed, "Gumbo!"

His old friend was about to get a front row seat to what an irate chef looked life. The new suppliers were proving to be worth their cheap prices.

"Gus! I need you in here right now!" Rafe moved toward the swinging doors. "We need to—"

The door swung in, smashing Rafe in the nose so hard blood spurted all over his white chef's coat.

Grabbing his face, he had no air left in his lungs to holler like he wanted to. Pain spread to the back of his head while stars sparked brightly behind his closed eyelids.

"Ah!" Rafe shouted, peering through the slits of his eyes to see the top of a red-haired head through the circle window.

Wrong color and too short to be Gus's.

Ever so slowly, the door crept open inch by inch until a woman could be seen holding it open with one slender hand. Her other hand reached toward him, as though she offered it to shake.

"Mr. Sinclair? I'm here to audition for your stage. But maybe I should come back at a different time." The woman cringed, eyeing his nose which felt doubled in size and still growing.

Rafe shook his head. With all the strength he could muster, he lifted his free hand, pointing to the front of the restaurant. "Out!"

Instead, the woman pushed past him and entered his domain, walking to the ice machine as though she owned the place. Lifting a white dish-towel from the rack, she scooped ice cubes into it, twisting the cloth to make an icepack. She brought it to his face but stopped short before touching him.

He met a pair of sharp amber eyes that quickly softened when she looked at his nose.

"I don't think it's broken," she said, removing his hand from his face. She turned his chin to study his nose from the side. "Nope. Just a lot of blood. Broken capillary."

"A singer who's a doctor?" Rafe deadpanned. "Is that part of your act?"

She bit her bright pink lower lip and dropped her gaze to his chest, now covered in blood. "Sorry about the coat. You can take it out of my first night's wages."

"That's not likely, since there won't be a first night." He ripped the ice from her hand and gently covered his throbbing nose. "Goodbye, *doc*."

The woman crossed her arms. "Mr. Sinclair, trust me when I tell you this. You need me."

"I need you to leave. Monroe, would you please escort this…*lady* to the door?" Rafe had a few other words to use but controlled his tongue.

Monroe smirked. "I don't know, boss. Maybe we should listen to her sing first. What's your name, mam?"

"Roxie Moon. I'm sure you've heard of me."

"No, we haven't," Rafe said. "And I don't need a

singer. I need a server. And judging by the pain in my nose, you already failed that audition, too."

"Perhaps we can talk about this in your office." She moved further into his kitchen. His office was at the rear of the room, but he sprang into action to block her at the end of the counter. She stepped to the side.

So did he.

"Who are you?" Rafe demanded, never feeling so annoyed by someone's presence. It was as though she considered herself in charge.

"I already told you. Roxie Moo—"

"No. Who sent you? Was it Morelli? Are you a spy sent to take me out completely?" Rafe wouldn't put it past his biggest competitor to send in the pretty redheaded songbird to steal his recipes and put them out on the internet.

The woman's demeanor changed from bullish to secretive instantly. She bit her lower lip again with her eyes downcast. "I don't know what you mean."

"I knew it. You can turn right around and tell Tony Morelli he messed with the wrong chef this time."

"I just want to sing." She looked over her shoulder at Monroe, who winked at her.

"Come on, boss, what could one song hurt?"

Rafe glared at his chef, sending the man back to chopping onions.

"Please, Mr. Sinclair. I can wait tables and do bookkeeping, too. You won't be disappointed. Here, let me show you." The woman belted out the start of a show tune right in his face.

Rafe gripped his head. "Stop. Please, just stop."

She ceased her singing, which wasn't bad but loud.

Monroe cleared his throat, holding up his paring knife. "How are you with a knife, Miss Moon?"

The woman's amber eyes widened, and her lips curled just a smidge. She resembled a cheshire cat. "A precision like you've never seen."

Rafe's next words locked in his throat. Why did her response feel...dangerous?

"I could use some help, Rafe." The pantry/sous chef/dishwasher waved his knife at that night's ingredients needing to be prepped. "You know you can't stay open for much longer without more employees."

"I can't pay them," Rafe admitted under his breath. He tested his nose for any more dripping blood. At the woman, he said, "Sorry, but you have to go."

"I'll work for free...I mean, until business picks

up. If I bring people in, I'll earn a commission. Something like that."

Monroe whistled. "You can't turn down that offer."

"See? Listen to him," she said, pleading with folded hands.

Rafe's head hurt, and it wasn't from the bruised nose. "You're awfully pushy. There can only be one head chef in the kitchen. Do you understand?"

"You're the boss. Where should I start?"

Rafe waved toward the dining room. "Ask Gus to put you to work."

"Gus?"

"Yeah, the man you saw when you came in."

Roxie frowned. "I didn't see anyone."

"What?" Rafe headed for the swinging doors, pushing through to find the dining room empty. "Gus?" he called as he checked the men's room.

Nothing.

Rafe checked the front entrance, looking down the snowy street. Perhaps he went out to shovel. At first, he saw no sign of his friend, but then he caught sight of two men turning the corner.

"There he is. He had a bill to mail. Must have gone to the post office." Rafe wondered who Gus walked with. The unknown man wore a wool coat with the collar turned up. He looked like one of Nico Rossi's men, but it made little sense for Gus to be chummy with the enemy.

Rafe was concerned but turned to face Roxie, only to find her now gone. He stood alone in the dining room wondering why she ran off. "Now, where did *she* go?"

Apparently, the pretty songbird also did a disappearing act.

CHAPTER 2

"*T*angen, we have a problem," Vera whispered into her phone from Creare's ladies' room. She locked the door behind her and slipped into one of the three stalls. Past etchings came through newly painted metal walls with one note off to her left that stated the chef was hot.

Rafe Sinclair was in a lot of hot water, that was for sure. *But okay, fine.* The man did curl her toes a bit. The idea of him working with Nico Rossi on the next heist disappointed her. Rafe didn't strike her as a mob guy, but she had heard Rossi say through the bug she'd planted on him that Creare would cooperate and assist in the heist.

"There's trouble already?" her handler responded. "Do I need to send a team to get you out?"

Vera was grateful for her handler and team, knowing all she had to do was say the word, and they would be there in seconds. But she had prepared for this day and wasn't giving up yet.

"I can do this. You know that. You trained me well. Just be on the ready. There's more to this place than we thought. Nico Rossi isn't just using it for his next heist. I just witnessed one of his goons walking with Gus Vargas, who apparently works here, though I can't fathom why. He's loaded. But isn't Paul Vargus Nico's number one enemy? Why would Gus Vargus, his son, be here? And friendly with a Rossi goon?"

A low whistle came through the phone's speaker. "What does Mr. Sunshine's heir to the Sunshine Hotels have to do with this heist?"

"I have no idea. But my cover could be blown. What if he heard about Roxie Moon? I could be walking out there to a disaster. I should have gone with a different identity."

"Where are you now?"

"I'm hiding out in the bathroom, and he's most likely in the restaurant now. I should have disappeared through the back entrance."

"You want to abort?"

Vera rubbed her forehead as she considered her next move. Being undercover as Roxie Moon would be too dangerous. Or would it?

"Let me think about this for a second. The Vargas family is supposed to be the number one enemy of the Rossi family. They will know Nico was duped by Roxie Moon just a week ago. They won't know yet she is FBI, right?"

"True. As of right now, Roxie Moon made Nico Rossi a laughingstock in his corner of the world. The Vargas family may think of her as an ally. But you mentioned you saw Gus with one of Nico's men. It sounds like the mob boss has a mole in his own entourage. Perhaps the snitch is trying to switch over to the Vargas family's string of businesses. They've been harder to crack than any of the Italian Mafia. Gambling, racketeering, auto theft, and the likes is a lot easier to break than their chain of hotels and restaurants. I can only assume Sinclair is looking to sell to them."

"Not yet. I didn't get that feeling when I spoke briefly with Sinclair. He's too clean."

"How do you know? If he's in the likes with the Vargas family, any of his dealings would be wiped clean. Let me do some fast digging on their connection."

Vera thought of the handsome curly-haired chef who now sported a swollen nose because of her entrance on the scene. Her lips twitched at how she nearly messed up this entire case from all angles. She had spent a week investigating the man, unbeknownst to him, digging into his colorful past. How he kept his list of women straight was beyond her. But other than that, he never left the kitchen. Cooking was his life since growing up in some rough neighborhoods of the city.

"Let me know what you find out," she replied. "I may have rushed coming in here. Vargas was not listed as an employee, and he's not someone who needs to be working under the table. His family owns a slew of restaurants manned by their own employees. His connection with Sinclair has got to be personal."

"So, either Sinclair is not as clean as you think, or Vargas isn't as dirty as we believe."

"He's filthy."

"Exactly." Tangen gulped something, most likely the black coffee that he poured into his veins daily. The man was ten years her senior, an associate deputy director of the FBI who dedicated his life's work to taking down the Rossi family. When Vera came to the Bureau, he'd singled her out as an ally. She had proven her worth to the man, and he'd taken her under his wing. They both had their reasons for wanting to take down Nico Rossi. Tangen's motive had something to do with an old partner who turned to the dark side under Rossi's tutelage and bribery. Vera didn't question Tangen's vendetta and vice versa. It made them a good team. "Gus Vargas is a suspected felon. You may believe Sinclair is innocent, completely ignorant of the dealings of his friends, but believing this will only put you in jeopardy. Here are the facts, Vera. The last heist that the Rossi family pulled off, a woman in her eighties was pushed down a flight of stairs and cracked her skull, killing her instantly. That bank robbery took place adjacent to one of the Vargas family's restaurants. Now you're telling me a Rossi goon is chummy with Gus Vargas. Coincidence? I think not."

"No such thing as coincidences." Vera unlatched the bathroom stall and approached the mirror. Roxie Moon stared back at her with no hint of the FBI agent beneath her façade. Even her striking amber eyes were fake, covered with colored contacts to mask her blues.

"Are you up for your biggest performance yet? From the looks of it, you'll be stuck between two crime families. You can't just take one down now. It's all or nothing. Once things go south, you will need evidence on both families to take them out before they take you out. And I don't mean on a date. Are you prepared to use every resource at your disposal?"

"Always...and yes, slipping into my undercover identities was never the problem. This will be Roxie Moon at her best."

Tangen chuckled. "God help them."

"No. They don't deserve God's help." The memory of identifying her parents' bodies at the morgue flashed through her mind. Something no child of any age should ever have to go through. At that time in her life, she relied on God for everything, aways walking by faith. After that night, she vowed to rely only on herself and her skills—and the 9 mm gun in her boot. "They need to pay for their crimes."

"They will, dear." Tangen sobered and his voice lowered. "All right. You know what you're looking for."

"Yes, sir." Vera recollected Nico Rossi's secret

meeting the week before. As far as she knew, he still didn't know a chip had been put into his pocket. His coat most likely had been sent to the cleaners the next day. But the intel she listened to spoke of their next heist on New Year's Eve. Rossi ordered 50 pounds of C-4 from the black market to be delivered to Creare. That was enough explosives to blow up a whole series of banks. Or the whole block. With the amount of people who came to the city for New Year's Eve, they could be looking at a catastrophic loss of life.

If only the man had hinted at the place that this would all go down.

What was the target?

What was Rossi's plan?

How could she alone stop something so enormous?

But I'm not alone. I have Tangen nearby. And I have Roxie. In fact, I have a whole satchel full of personalities at my disposal. Vera was certain not even Tangen knew the real Vera Sharp. Vera wasn't sure she would even recognize her anymore, either.

Or if she wanted to.

Entering the FBI had been more than for retribution. It was also a place to hide. A life of undercover personalities, changing from one to another, kept her real identity in the shadows. It gave her distance from people emotionally.

Tangen brought Vera back with his direction. "We wait for that delivery. If all goes well, it will give us all we need to convict everyone involved before anyone gets hurt. You'll need to move fast and make sure all parties are revealed."

"I already told Sinclair that I can do the book-keeping. A paper trail will be my first attempt. But I'll need a file on Vargas. Everything you can get me. Who his head of security is and any criminal history. But most particularly, I want to know who he is to Rafe Sinclair."

"Already on it."

A knock wrapped at the door. "Are you in there, Roxie?" Rafe's voice bellowed from the other side of the heavy wooden door.

Tangen said in her ear, "Keep me on the line."

Vera kept the phone in her palm at her side and called out, "Be right there!" The singsong voice of Roxie Moon spilled from Vera's lips without hesitance. Her personas could be turned on and off like a switch. She could be Roxie at one moment and then Winifred Winterbottom in the same sentence. Vera smiled remembering her old-wealthy, octogenarian identity she used last year to take down an embezzler in an oil company.

Under her breath, she whispered in her best crackly Winnie voice, "I'm on my way, you little whippersnapper. You thought you knew a lot of women before. You're about to meet a whole phonebook full, including a few men, when the need arises."

Vera cleared her throat and swung the door wide. "Did you miss me?"

Rafe stood with his arms folded in front of him. "Give me one reason why I don't fire you right now?"

Vera stepped close and rested her hand on his chest. "I'm pretty sure you don't need a reason, but I'm also pretty sure you know I'm your last shot at saving your restaurant."

"Gus doesn't agree." He grabbed her hand and pushed her away. "Come with me. He wants to meet you."

"Fabulous." Vera followed Rafe to the dining room, staying behind him to shield her face until she could survey her surroundings. Gus Vargas stood at the host station looking at a computer screen and, thankfully, Nico's goon was nowhere in sight.

But would Gus recognize her, anyway? Of all her personalities, why had she chosen Roxie?

"Here she is," Rafe announced. "Creare's newest server, bookkeeper, singer, whatever. She's a Jill of all trades, I guess you could say. What would you like her to do first?"

Gus kept his attention on the computer screen. Yet to look up, he typed as he spoke. "The dining room is ready for tonight, so why don't you sing for us?"

Vera sent a quick look at Rafe, who seemed smug with a suppressed smile. Was he setting her up? She weighed her next move carefully. Was it better to give a good performance or a bad one?

Then she remembered Tangen asking her if she was up for her best performance yet?

Vera noticed the stage that had a large round table in the center for a big party. Slowly, she made her way over to climb the two steps and stand at the front. She cradled her phone in her hand with Tangen still on the line, tucking it behind her thigh as she lifted her chin and released the first notes of an Italian soprano aria from *Madame Butterfly*.

The intimate and warming lyrics sung by Butterfly in the opera tells the story that one beautiful day after so long, her long lost love would find his way back to her. A puff of smoke on the horizon would reveal his return, and they would be together again.

Vera held nothing back. Every muscle in her body worked to push the song out from deep within her. At some point, her eyes closed, and she *was* Butterfly. Never had she felt so raw and unhidden as she did at the culmination of the aria. When she opened her eyes, the room blurred through her tears, and as she wiped them away, she noticed where there had been two men before five more now stood in front of her. Rafe and Gus had been joined by Monroe who also had tears streaming down his cheeks. Four other strangers stood at the entrance, two women and two men, their mouths gaped wide.

Gus spoke first, seemingly in a daze. "Um…we're not open."

Rafe glanced his friend's way. "Of course we are. Please, won't you come sit?" He rushed toward the four people at the door, snatching menus from the host station as he moved forward. "Monroe, please take their coats."

Monroe swiped at his cheeks and rushed forward to do as he was told. He hung the coats on the hooks on the wall by their table and ran back to the kitchen.

"Can we be closer to the stage?" one of the women asked.

"Absolutely," Rafe said and moved up two tables. "This is Roxie Moon, Creare's talent tonight...and every night."

Vera took the first step down. "We need to talk."

"After your first set is done." Rafe stopped her from descending any further. His sharp blue topaz eyes locked on hers, and he mouthed, "Thank you."

If he didn't have tears in his eyes before, he definitely did now. A look of gratitude shimmered her way, only magnified with a look of hope. Gone was the angry, dejected chef she met only an hour ago.

Had her song done that?

"I need a few minutes," Vera implored him.

"Water? Let me get you a bottle." Rafe turned back for the host station. "Gus, hand me a fresh bottle."

"Rafe, we can't hire her," Gus barely shielded his voice. He handed a bottle to Rafe.

"We'll talk about that later."

"You asked me to help you keep the doors open. Roxie Moon isn't the way you want to go. Trust me." Rafe turned his back and twisted the cap off.

Vera stepped down to the floor to reach for the drink. With a trembling hand, she poured half of it down her throat, realizing she still clutched the phone in her other hand. This wasn't how being undercover was supposed to be. She was supposed to be detached from her identities; unaffected by them.

But never had she felt so connected...so close to her true self.

Vera Sharp was supposed to be hidden at all times.

"I'll be right back." Vera made her way to the restrooms, her knees a bit wobbly. In the hallway, she lifted the phone to her ear. "Did you hear all that?" she whispered.

"Well done, my dear. You're in. Now go get 'em. Every last one of them." With her handler's orders in place, she heard the line go dead.

"Roxie Moon is going to save me." Rafe laid out four plates across the stainless-steel counter for the four new diners awaiting their meals. He turned for the stove and picked up the ladle, giving Gus his back. As far as Rafe was concerned, the conversation was over.

Gus approached from the left, apparently not in agreement. "You know nothing about this woman. She could be a plant from Tony Morelli. Have you even considered that?"

"Of course I did. That was the first thought I had." Rafe spooned basmati rice onto two of the plates. "But if Tony was dumb enough to let Roxie Moon go, I say his loss is my gain. Listen to her. Her voice is like nothing I've ever heard. It gets me right here." Rafe touched his chest, then pointed at Gus. "Don't mess this up on me. You wanted to help me? Start by letting the world know about her. Although she's bringing in anyone walking by."

Roxie's current song filtering through the swinging doors was another aria in her second set. He considered propping the doors open so he and Monroe wouldn't miss a note.

"Too much publicity too fast could lead to destruction if you can't keep up with it. What if she doesn't show up tomorrow and there's a full dining room?"

Rafe spooned out the medallions on the plates and bent to place the garnish of julienne radishes on the side. He handed two plates to Gus and picked up the remaining meals, expecting his friend to follow him out. At the door, he turned back. "Once they're in the door, it's my job to see they come back. Are you saying you don't believe in me? In my cooking?" He hit the doors with his elbows, swinging them wide, and brought the meals out for the diners.

Two other tables now were filled. He placed the meals down at the first table, taking the other two from Gus, and was careful not to disturb the customers' concentration on Roxie. He moved to a second table and quietly took their order. Passing the third table, he assured them he would be right back. The guests were so enamored with Roxie that all they did was nod. Rafe couldn't blame them. At the swinging doors, he turned to watch her sing.

She was smooth...and stunning. Maybe it was the throbbing nose on his face when he first met her that blinded him to just how pretty she was. But there was no denying it now. She took his breath away.

But nothing could happen between them.

Rafe knew his track record with women never went beyond two weeks, and he never parted as friends. Only once had there been someone who he believed would be for life. Once was one too many times for him. He learned quickly it was best to have a few fun dates and be on his way.

But he couldn't lose Roxie Moon, and that meant hands off.

He closed his eyes and absorbed the melody from her lips into his whole being. It warmed him even as goosebumps popped out on his skin's surface. On a sigh, he opened his eyes and found her watching him. He knew he should return to the kitchen and start the orders, but he couldn't have moved a muscle even if he wanted to. It was as though she sang just for him.

But that was crazy. He'd been in New York City long enough to know show business was all about making the audience feel the show was just for them. And Roxie Moon was a pro at it.

"I'm worried about you," Gus said close to his ear.

Rafe hadn't realized his friend had even approached him. Maybe Gus was right to be worried. He clapped Gus on the back. "Duly noted. But you don't have to worry about me. She's one that I'll love from afar."

"Love?" Gus sputtered.

Rafe cracked a smile and turned for the swinging doors. "Kidding, buddy. It was a joke. That ship sailed a long time ago. You know that."

"Right. You had me going there for a second. The self-proclaimed bachelor Rafael Sinclair, chef extraordinaire, can't fall in love. You remember what happened the last time."

Ray frowned. "Yeah, nearly ruined me. Thanks to you, my life was saved. I will never forget that, Gumbo. And now you're here, doing it again. You're the best."

Rafe hit the doors, and for the next three hours, had the busiest night in months, cooking and preparing his best meals that gave him his super chef stardom years ago. For the first time in over a year, Rafe believed he could get it back.

Hours later, everyone had gone home for the night, leaving Rafe to close up. He entered his office at the back of the kitchen and tallied the night's earnings. Three times he crunched the numbers, unsure if he was missing receipts. The income came to half of what he expected. In his mind, he counted the number of meals he served and thought drinks and desserts had also been ordered. Perhaps he was mistaken. As successful as the night had been, it wouldn't be enough to save him.

Rafe closed the ledger on the computer and powered down. He picked up his coat draped on the arm of the small sofa and hit the lights in his office and then the kitchen. He made his way to the rear exit and locked up behind him. Parked in the back lot by the dumpster was his blue Porsche. He had thought he would have to sell it soon. He climbed in but didn't start the engine. Instead, he sat for a few minutes in the dark and let the emotional memory of the night soothe his nerves. It amazed him how one woman had the power to do this.

All it took was a pretty songbird to give him hope again.

The screech of a cat somewhere down the alley pulled his attention and caused him to cringe. The harsh sound was a 180 from Roxie's warm and inviting soprano.

As if he conjured her up just thinking about her, above the hood of his car, he saw her standing there.

Rafe opened the door and jumped out. "I thought you left with everyone. Is everything all right?"

"I came back." He could hear tears in her voice, and he rushed to her side. "We need to talk. Rafe, I don't think—"

"Stop. Don't say anything else. Whatever is bothering you, we'll work it out." He took her by the arm and led her to the passenger side of his car. He opened the door and invited her to sit. Circling the rear of the car, he climbed back behind the driver's seat and started the engine. "Where to?"

Instantly, Roxie dropped her head into her hands and burst into tears. Heart wrenching sobs filled the small cabin of his sports car, making him feel useless to soothe her after she had just spent the entire evening comforting others.

"Tell me. How can I help you?" Rafe asked, fumbling with his hands as he reached for her knee. "I mean it when I say this. Roxie, I take care of what is mine, and after tonight, that includes you. You are a part of Creare. How can I help you?"

"I don't have a place to go. My roommate kicked me out. Would it be okay if I slept here? In your office?"

"Here?"

"I'm sure you've slept here before."

Rafe sought a response to negate her words but came up empty. "Well, yes, but not by choice. There's a loveseat in the office, but it's not very comfortable."

"It will just be for tonight. Tomorrow, I'll find a place. I promise."

Rafe thought about bringing Roxie back to his apartment but only let that thought last for two seconds. He reminded himself of his hands-off promise from earlier that evening. There was no way he would ruin this ticket back to his success.

He cut the engine and opened the doors, first to the car and then to his restaurant. He unlocked his office and led her inside. Roxie immediately dropped to the loveseat, looking deflated.

"Can I get you something to eat? I would have fed you tonight, but you left so fast after your third set."

"I got a text from my roommate. I had to rush home. Things were going down fast."

Rafe pulled up his office chair and fell back into it. "I'm sorry. I was so focused on the business you were bringing in that I neglected to see you were dealing with other things. Important things. Obviously, you needed a job. You even told me you wanted to talk. Can you forgive me?"

Roxie tilted her head, allowing her red waves to cascade into her lap. "Forgive you? There's nothing to forgive. You're so different than…never mind."

Rafe leaned forward with his elbows on his knees. "Different than what?

A sweet blush spread across her face. She dropped her gaze to her fidgeting hands in her lap. "Well, it's been my experience that most men would take advantage of me in this situation. But you just want to feed me." She lifted a dazzling smile. "I misjudged you, Mr. Sinclair."

"Rafe." He leaned back, not having the heart to tell her the thought had crossed his mind, and he had to make himself a promise. "Some things are too valuable to mishandle."

Her lips trembled before she pressed them tight. She eyed the kitchen. "You wouldn't happen to have some of that amazing white truffle pasta left, would you? My mouth was watering when I saw it on that young couple's plates tonight."

"Coming right up. And I'll be sure to keep extras on hand for you from now on."

"You're too good to me."

"Right back atcha."

All the while, prepping her food, Rafe found his cheeks ached from the huge smile on his face. As he returned to the office with her heaping plate of pasta, he found her watching him from the door. He handed her the plate.

"You are a master, but I suppose you've been told that before." She took the sofa again, but this time moved as far over as possible. "Sit with me and help me eat some of this. It's way too much for me, and you did cook it, after all."

Rafe hesitated, his gaze studying the empty

cushion next to her. Why did this feel like a test? And why did he already know he was going to fail it?

"I'm not coming on to you. If I was, you would know it," she said sweetly.

He cracked a smile. "Oh yeah, how so?"

"I have the worst pickup lines."

"Let me guess…lines like 'you wouldn't happen to have some of that amazing white truffle pasta left, would you?'"

Roxie threw her head back in a full, gleeful laugh. "That was pathetic, wasn't it? But it wasn't a lie." She picked up the fork and dug in, slurping up the long fettucine with full abandon and delight. "This is soooo good."

Roxie exuded pure beauty as she devoured his food, and Rafe knew he was in for the test of his life.

CHAPTER 3

"*I*f you were president, you'd be Babe-raham Lincoln."

Vera groaned. "All right, you win. That is the worst pickup line I've ever heard. Please tell me no one has fallen for that." Vera let her head fall back to the top of the cushion, stifling a fake yawn, hoping Rafe was falling for her own act.

He held up his hand and turned to face her. His knee bumped hers, and she didn't move out of the way. She kept her knee still, touching his, letting him get used to her closeness. She kind of felt bad for making him think there was anything between them. It was the nature of the beast with her job. To get intel, she had to use people and lead them along. She reminded herself that this was to take down Nico Rossi and it would all be worth it in the end.

"You'd be surprised. What part didn't you like? Was it the part where I said babe?"

"No. It was the fact you insinuated I couldn't be president with my own name." Vera raised her eyebrows, feigning offense.

Rafe winced. "Right. Never thought of that. I'll remember next time."

Vera gawked. "You mean you're going to use it again?"

Rafe shrugged, suppressing a grin. "If the situation fits. But after tonight I'll remember white truffle pasta will also work."

Vera glanced at the empty plate on his desk. "You are a fabulous chef. Stick with that when it comes to the ladies."

Rafe glanced down to where their knees touched and grew quiet. Vera waited for him to put his hand on her knee and make a move. It would show she had earned his trust, and she could begin the questions she held back on her tongue.

"Do you want to tell me what happened with your roommate?"

That was *not* what Vera was expecting from him. His long list of girlfriends said he never passed on making a pass. "Is this one of your pickup lines?" She laughed, hearing a bit of unease in her voice that wasn't faked.

He did not laugh. Instead, he moved his knee away from hers and faced forward. Brushing his thighs with his palms, he sighed. "I understand if you don't want to share. It's none of my business. I just want you to know I'm here if you need to talk." Rafe stood and reached for the door. "I'll let you get some sleep." He frowned, looking at the sofa. "As much as one can on that thing. What am I doing?" He patted the front of his white chef pants, then reached behind him. Withdrawing a black wallet, he pulled out a collection of bills. "Let me give you money for a hotel."

"No." Vera jumped to her feet. Nothing was going the way she thought it would.

"It's the least I can do after you saved me tonight. Consider it an advance on your pay."

"No, really. I don't want your money." Vera pushed away the cash he held out to her. "I'll be fine here. It's just one night. I'll be gone by morning to look for a new place. Don't worry about me, Rafe."

"I *will* worry about you. And it's got nothing to do with you saving Creare tonight."

Vera tilted her head coyly. This was what she was

waiting for, her open door to step into. "No? Why do you care so much?"

"I don't."

"Oh."

"I'm worried someone will steal you from me. There are constant threats of theft in the culinary underbelly. Recipes, customers, and even the talent. You are mine now. Understand?"

"That's the second time you've said that. *Mine*. I don't think I like that."

He leaned close, causing Vera to hold still. He lifted his hand to her face but didn't touch her. His hand hovered inches away.

"Get used to it because it's true. You will be the face of Creare. Good night...*Butterfly*."

Vera stood still, long after Rafe had left the office and locked up the rear exit. She had played this evening all wrong. Tangen had been right about Rafe Sinclair. He wasn't as innocent as Vera believed. He kept company with crime lords, after all. Of course, he would know about their lifestyle. And most likely be a part of the crimes. How could she overlook that and believe him to be an innocent victim and the weakest link in the investigation? She also believed him to be a man easily conned by a few flirtations? He was a successful forty-five-year-old bachelor chef with multiple little black books. He'd been around the block more times than could be counted. He'd seen every tactic played out to grab his attention and used them on others as well. He had to know she was playing the damsel in distress for a reason.

And he rejected her flat.

But worse, he put her in her place instantly. The message was loud and clear: *You are mine now. Understand?*

Vera thought of calling Tangen. But he would only say that he told her so. Then he would remind her to get back to work. It was less than four weeks until New Year's Eve, and fifty pounds of C-4 was set to blow.

So Rafe Sinclair was *out* as the *in* she needed to crack the case. Who next? Monroe? *Nah*. The pantry chef won't know anything but what's on the menu. So, did she go straight to Gus Vargas?

The man already didn't trust her, and it wouldn't be long before he figured out that she had duped Nico a week ago. He most likely already had his men investigating Roxie Moon.

Her time here was short. She needed evidence of the next heist, enough to convict Rossi and anyone else involved. Then it was time for her to fly and

Tangen and his team to move in. She provided the intel and evidence and never revealed her identity. Get in, get out, was her part.

But if she wanted to cuff Rossi, that would need to change with this case.

Vera pulled on her photographic memory of Gus's file that Tangen sent over earlier that evening. Mr. Sunshine's son and heir to the hotel and restaurant chains appeared to have a whistle-clean history. He attended the Culinary Institute of America with Rafe twenty-five years ago, but their relationship went back five years before that. Rafe worked for his father at a bistro on 9th Avenue, down in Hell's Kitchen. Gus and Rafe became close friends, and it was Papa Vargas who paid for both their tuitions. Rafe agreed to work for the Vargas family for ten years. As soon as his time was up, he bought into Creare, along with two women, Melody Mesini and Christina DePalo, both married and out of the picture now. Vera didn't see either woman in Rafe's file as ever being one of his liaisons. Judging by his self-control with her tonight, perhaps she misjudged him when it came to women. Not everyone in his life was added to his little black books.

What had he just said to her?

Some things are too valuable to mishandle.

So, Rafe recognized boundaries when something was important to him. Mel and Chris were obviously important to him.

Vera circled the office, taking in the few photos on the wall and on the top of the desk. Rafe was in most of them, and so was Gus. There was one photo with just Rafe and two women on either side of him. Recalling the images of Mel and Chris from their files, Vera identified them as Rafe's business partners. They seemed close, and with his arm on either of their shoulders, he obviously valued them. Though, the look he gave Mel said he may have thought more of her than as friends. Maybe she would ask them someday but probably not. Vera had more pressing matters to attend to than Rafe's past loves.

The other photos with Gus fell under more urgency. The two had been friends for a long time. Had they ever had a falling out? Once again, she thought of Rafe's words about protecting what was valuable. Gus obviously fell under that umbrella. But that didn't mean Rafe was as important to Gus. After all, what could Gus need from Rafe that the man couldn't buy himself? What made their friendship last so long? What did Rafe bring to the table? The logical answer would be giving Gus a front for his family's illegal crimes.

Perhaps Rafe's ten years never ended, except on paper. Vera didn't know too many crime families that put a time limit on someone's indentured service. Typically, when someone's time was up, their heart conveniently stopped as well.

She glanced at the computer, not giving it a second thought. She would be wasting her time trying to hack in. Plus, Tangen could hack in and easily get what the team needed and probably already tried. There would be nothing to find there.

Vera moved to the filing cabinet but found all five drawers locked. She reached under her wig and pulled out one of the bobby pins keeping her blond hair hidden. Twenty seconds later, she had the first file unlocked and pulled wide. Tax returns, food orders, employee applications…everything appeared to be in order. If the IRS came knocking, Rafe would pass with flying colors.

And yet Rossi was using Creare for his next heist.

A creaking sound from the kitchen alerted Vera. Her hand paused on the handle of the second door. Had Rafe returned in the middle of the night? Maybe he never left and was watching to be sure she didn't take off or rob him blind.

Or did she have other company?

An impromptu meeting with Gus could be premature and mess up everything.

Vera crouched low and removed the gun from her boot. She'd keep it hidden in the folds of her dress until she knew if the visitor had unlawful ideas up their sleeve. She stepped up behind the door and waited for another sound. When none came, she wondered if she imagined it. Perhaps it was the heating vent coming on or the motor of the walk-in freezer next door. She let herself relax her stance.

Then a clatter erupted from the kitchen. It sounded like someone had knocked over the pots and pans in the washroom. But it definitely was a person and not the heating or cooling systems.

Had Monroe returned to wash dishes?

Vera checked her phone for the time.

Two a.m.

Who does that? The man deserved a raise, and she planned to tell Rafe to give him one in the morning. Vera questioned if she should alert Monroe, or whoever the dishwasher was, to her presence. But she didn't want to give them a heart attack by sneaking up on them.

Then all went quiet again—until the office doorknob turned slowly.

Vera rolled her eyes and readied herself to knock someone out. It would be a hit first, ask questions later situation. She'd have to claim ignorance and fear tomorrow when asked why she hit someone, but she couldn't blow her cover with skilled martial arts, even if a few moves would be the easiest resource— and even if she'd love to interrogate her visitor.

The door opened, and Vera raised the butt of her gun. In the dim light of the lamp on the desk, she immediately saw black curls.

Rafe.

Vera lowered her gun back to her side. "Didn't trust me?" she asked.

Rafe swung around on a gasp, facing her with eyes wide in shock. Only it *wasn't* Rafe at all. Just someone who looked like him.

A much younger version of him.

"You're not Rafe," Vera said, mentally cycling through all the files of people in Rafe's life that she had studied that week. She never saw this man in any of them.

"No," the stranger said. Vera put him at early to mid-twenties. He carried a heaping plate of the pasta. "I'm not Rafe. I'm his son." A southern lilt came through his voice.

"Liar." The word spilled from Vera's lips before she could stop it.

"Why do you say that?"

"Because I know everything about Rafe." Everything the file told her, anyway. Had Tangen left this crucial detail out on purpose? *Why?*

"Sorry to be the one to tell you, ma'am, but you don't know everything."

Vera didn't know which made her angrier: being called ma'am or learning important details had been kept from her.

She waved her gun toward the sofa. "That ends tonight. Sit down and start talking."

***

I'M IN TOWN.

That's all the text said.

Rafe rolled over and checked the clock. It was a few minutes before seven a.m., but the text came in at 1:30. That was a long time for trouble to ensue. He threw off his covers and readied quickly for the day and for whatever was on his plate.

Years as a good line cook had prepared him to remain clearheaded and reasonably even keeled in frantic kitchen settings, as well as with potential destruction outside in the real world.

Grady showing up here unannounced had catastrophic destruction written all over it. The boy better have a good excuse. Rafe sent off a response text.

Did you eat breakfast?

Because food was the only thing Rafe knew. Food had saved him from a life on the streets. Most people in the business wound up on the line because something in their lives had gone terribly wrong. Sure, there were artists in the business, and at one time Rafe had thought of himself in this category. Those were vain years Rafe would like to forget. Now, cooking was about the craft and about the relationships that ingredients brought together. It was a lesson Rafe learned too late. But he also learned who he could trust to handle the things he wasn't good at.

Rafe dialed the phone, waiting for Gus to pick up as he headed out of his apartment and down to the lobby.

"A little early, don't you think?" a groggy voice answered.

"Grady's in town. I'm meeting him at the restaurant."

"Why?"

"Because that's the safest place to meet him."

"No. Why is he in town?" An edge of panic laced Gus's words.

"I don't know. It's Christmas time. Maybe he felt like celebrating with his old man."

"Rafe. It's not safe to meet him anywhere." Gus lowered his voice to a near whisper. "The kid looks just like you. It won't take a genealogy expert to know who belongs to. Rossi will figure it out. You're willing to throw everything we worked for away? What would Angela say?"

Rafe frowned at the sound of Angela's name, his first love taken from this world so soon when all she wanted to was to raise their little family...and keep her father from finding out about Grady. The idea of Rossi learning that his daughter had a son turned Rafe's stomach.

"I'll send him home. Today. I just wanted to let you know in case you had a better idea of what to do with them. You helped me find him a good home and keep his existence a secret."

Gus sighed through the phone, and Rafe could picture him dragging his hand across his face. "Just tell him...tell him his uncle Gus says Merry Christmas."

Rafe stepped out onto the street and hopped into his Porsche. "Will do. I'll keep it short and sweet."

"Yeah, do that before anyone else sees him. At least he knew enough to show up during the night and not during working hours."

"We've taught him well. I'll have him gone before Monroe shows—shoot." Rafe hit the steering wheel and peeled out into the traffic.

"That didn't sound good. What's going on?"

"I let Roxie sleep in the office last night. She got booted from her apartment. There's no way the two of them haven't met yet."

Gus groaned, the decibel getting louder by the second. "We know nothing about her. She could be a plant. And you just handed her our one and only bargaining chip."

"My son is not a bargaining chip, and how was I supposed to know he would show up the same night she would be there? Don't worry about it. She's not a plant."

"How do you know?"

Rafe thought of his time with Roxie the night before. There was definitely something about her that made him uneasy, but she was too driven to be working for anyone but herself. He recognized himself in her a bit. He also recognized the bit of

Mel and Chris in her, and that meant she needed to be protected. She could be taken advantage of too easily.

"She's just like me. She's an underdog, trying to make it in this world without being corrupted and stay true to herself." Rafe said. "Spend five minutes with her, and you'll agree."

"If she sticks around for more than two weeks, I'll consider it."

"She will. I won't let her leave. She's going to save Creare."

Gus laughed. "Something tells me Roxie Moon doesn't take orders and will do as she pleases."

Rafe pulled up to the restaurant and took the street next to it to pull into his back lot parking space. "Yes, but she'll learn she's stronger with our support. Now, if you'll excuse me, I have to head into Creare to see what transpired between her and Grady."

"This could be very bad. What if Rossi's men came sniffing around this morning like one of his men did yesterday? I think we're being watched for some reason. Rossi might offer to buy again."

"The answer is still no."

"Rossi doesn't like that."

"We'll deal with it then. Right now, Grady is my

only concern." Rafe disconnected the call, locked his car, and headed inside.

"Roxie? Grady?" Rafe called out into the dimly lit kitchen. He opened his office door to find it empty. He checked the walk-in freezer and refrigerator just to cross it off the list. Making his way through the double swinging doors, he found the dining room just as desolate and the bathrooms empty.

They were both gone.

Rafe checked his phone, realizing Grady never responded to him after Rafe asked him if he ate breakfast.

What if Rossi's men had shown up here this morning? What would they have done to the two of them? Grady would never see the light of day again, that much Rafe knew. Just as Gus had said, everything they'd done to protect him from his grandfather would have been for nothing. Every sacrifice made to give him a better life would be worthless and wasted.

Rafe pushed the thought aside. Even if Rossi got his hands on Grady, it wouldn't change his son's character. He would still be the strong, moralistic young man he was raised to be. He would still be the person his mother dreamed he could be.

A muffled, deep laugh filtered Rafe's way. A

glance through the glass showed Grady and Roxie huddled together in the cold as a gust of wind picked up, pushing them forward. Grady opened the door, holding it wide for her, and when they both stood in front of Rafe, they halted.

"Good morning," Rafe said, folding his arms. "Don't the two of you look chummy."

The two looked at each other, and in the next second, erupted with a burst of laughter. Rafe gave them a minute to get themselves under control.

"Roxie, I need to speak with this young man alone," Rafe said. "Would you mind waiting in my office?"

"It's okay, Rafe. She knows everything," Grady said, wrapping an arm around her shoulders.

"I hope you're joking," Rafe said. Had the boy forgotten how dangerous it would be for the wrong people to find out about him?

Roxie stepped forward and put her hand on Rafe's forearm. "He explained it all. How you let his birth mother give him up for adoption, not interfering with her decision. That was brave of both of you."

That wasn't the whole truth, but it would do.

Rafe glanced at Grady, who only nodded once for

Rafe to agree with the story. Perhaps his son was smarter than he let on.

"Right. It was for the best. I was in no place to raise a baby myself," Rafe repeated the line that he had practiced for twenty-five years. He reached to tap the insignia of the boy's university on his coat. "Private school. Ivy League college. As you can see, Grady had nothing but the best."

Roxie raised her perfect eyebrows. "Except he didn't have his dad."

The comment packed a punch that Rafe hoped didn't give his guilt away. She couldn't understand why a decision like this had to be made, and he wasn't about to elaborate.

"It's okay, Roxie," Grady said. "I hold no grudges. At least not against Rafe."

Rafe searched his son's face for what his words meant. The tilt of the boy's set jaw raised the hair on the back of Rafe's neck. Was that the reason Grady was in town? A personal vendetta towards the person he did hold a grudge against? The reason he had to live a life under the radar?

There was only one man who fit that bill.

Nico Rossi.

"How long are you in town for, Grady?" Rafe didn't hide his displeasure at the impromptu visit.

"The holiday season is busy for me. I wish you would have called."

"And have you tell me not to come?" Grady waved his hand in the air, then locked his arm into Roxie's. "We do need to talk about you leaving this woman in your office, though. She nearly killed me."

"Killed you?"

Roxie laughed. "He's exaggerating. I carry a small weapon with me for protection. I thought he was breaking in."

"You carry a gun?"

"It's permitted."

"Still. That's something I would have liked to have known."

She shrugged coyly. "It never came up when you forced me on the stage."

"You had plenty of time after you showed up here after midnight last night."

"I was too busy being rejected."

Grady shook his head with a frown. "Rafe, we need to talk about your lack of skills in the dating department."

Rafe sputtered. "Lack of skills? *As if.* First of all, she's an employee. I don't cross that line. Second, and you of all people should know, it could be dangerous."

"Excuses, excuses," Roxie teased him, followed by a nervous laugh. "Why would it be dangerous? Are you afraid of me?"

"Terrified." Rafe sent Grady a look that said, *drop it.*

Thankfully, his boy was bright enough to deserve to get into an Ivy League school and read Rafe loud and clear. He nodded with a yawn and stretched his arms. "I'm beat. I'm heading to the hotel to get some sleep. Roxie—" Grady pulled her in tight for a side hug. "—keep in touch."

"You know how to reach me, sweetie," Roxie said with a pat to Grady's cheek. "But are you sure you can't stay longer? Are you really going to leave before Christmas?"

Grady glanced Rafe's way over Roxie's red hair. "We're not the holiday-celebrating kind of family. And if anyone ever asks you, we're not family at all."

"Who would I tell?"

Roxie's question hung between them in the empty dining room, feeling almost like a dare. It made Rafe question her innocence for a moment. Perhaps Gus was right to hold off trusting her just yet. What if she was a plant? She now knew his deepest secret and could destroy him.

Or worse, destroy Grady.

Rafe gripped his stomach where a wave of nausea settled, thick and unrelenting. He had to make sure she understood how devastating it would be if anyone found out. But how could Rafe do that without trusting her with more information?

First, Rafe needed to talk with Grady to find out why his son showed up here in the first place. He took a substantial risk, which meant something big was going on.

"You can't even tell your mama," Grady said, answering her question. Rafe noticed she frowned at his son's words. "Don't forget that, Roxie. And don't forget your promise you made to me."

It seemed Grady offered her trust right away as well. Rafe would have to talk to him about that when they had their little chat at the hotel. He watched his son exit and disappear into the city traffic. Time was short before Grady needed to disappear completely.

Right now, Roxie had to be dealt with.

"He's a good kid," she said with her back to him. Slowly, she turned and settled those amber eyes on him. "But imagine my surprise when he showed up here last night. I'm sorry if my presence threw a wrench into your little reunion. I really won't tell anyone. Though, I can't imagine why you're not proud of him, and why you wouldn't want to shout it from the rooftops that you're his father."

"Who said I didn't want that? There are some people who would take him from me. I don't expect you to understand, and I can't go into it with you without compromising him more. Can I really trust you to never breathe a word of this to anyone?"

She raised her right hand. "On my honor."

"Even under torture."

Her eyebrows arched in surprise, but she quickly nodded. "Nothing will happen to your son. I promise."

It wasn't a promise she could make, but Rafe appreciated the gesture.

"Great. Now show me the gun."

Roxie's eyebrows arched again while a small smile flitted across her lips. "I don't have any idea what you're talking about. Why would I have a gun? I wouldn't even know how to use it. I'd probably shoot my foot right off." With that, she turned and entered the kitchen, proving her ability to lie.

But would Rossi believe her lies?

CHAPTER 4

"*T*angen, we need to talk. Call me as soon as you get this message." Vera stepped off the rear exit stoop, clicked off, and pocketed her phone. Last night did not go as planned, and she wasn't any closer to finding a tie between Rafe's restaurant and Nico Rossi. What she did find was that her handler did not do his homework. Vera did not like being surprised when undercover. She never went in until she had memorized every minute detail about the people she would be investigating. She considered Rafe having a son—even one given up for adoption—a gargantuan detail.

What if she had killed Grady last night? The young man didn't even realize how close he had come to being knocked unconscious. That alone would have ruined the entire investigation. She nearly gave herself away by exposing her gun. Thankfully, the boy was more book smarts than street. He accepted her lame excuse for self-protection in the city, and they went on to enjoy a bagel and coffee like they were lifelong friends. The strange part was it actually seemed as though they were. Vera didn't even feel like she was acting.

Grady Andrews was a good kid. The promise she made to Rafe wasn't a lie. She would make sure the boy remained free of the tangled web Rossi had for Creare. It was good Grady was heading out of town today. The sooner the better.

Vera quickly passed by Rafe's dark blue Porsche. She now knew from his file that the 1982 vintage 911 Targa had been a generous gift after graduation from Mr. Sunshine. Along with Rafe's education paid for, it appeared Rafe owed Paul Vargas a lot. Perhaps all he had to do was look away when Mr. Sunshine needed Creare to run his crimes.

Vera made it to the front of the street just in time to see Grady turn the corner on the opposite block. She picked up her steps to not lose him, and after four more blocks, she wondered why he hadn't hailed a cab. Three blocks later and she was back to where she started.

The man was walking in circles.

What are you up to, Grady? Did he know she followed him?

Vera picked up her steps, racing along the icy streets. Her phone buzzed in her coat pocket, and she retrieved it while keeping her eyes on the black curls bouncing above the crowded streets.

"There you are," she said to Tangen. "I need everything on Rafe's son, Grady Andrews."

"Pardon me? Did you say, son?"

"He's twenty-five years old. Apparently, one of Rafe's liaisons when he was twenty had a baby, and she gave the boy up for adoption. I want to know everything about her as well."

"A little jealous, are you?"

Vera sputtered and didn't respond to such an accusation, even if Rafe's rejection of her the night before felt a little personal. And she didn't buy his excuse about not crossing that line with an employee. She read his file. He'd crossed it many times.

"I hope this will be your one and only faux pas," she said. "This complete case nearly blew up in my face last night. Don't let it happen again." She cut the line and pocketed her phone.

Grady took the next left, but when Vera turned the corner, he was gone.

I lost him? How?

She never lost her target. She ran at top speed to the next corner, looking left and right. Vera zigzagged her way through the hotdog line, under a haze of steam and through the scent of street meat. A bell jingled off in the distance in front of the post office. A man dressed as Santa stood at a red easel, asking for money in the name of good cheer.

As an FBI agent, Vera was trained for the unexpected. Yet, when she reached the jolly man, she wasn't expecting him to put out his foot. With her eyes looking for curly hair in the throngs of people, she missed the black boot, not realizing it until she sailed through the air.

Vera came down on the pavement hard, the wind in her lungs knocked clean out of her. It took her a moment to register what had just happened. "Ow." She pushed up on her hands, now cut and bleeding.

"Are you all right?" A woman kneeled before her.

Vera jumped to her feet, not willing to trust anyone. A glance back showed Santa Man was gone, leaving nothing but his easel and bell on the ground.

Now she looked for two people, vowing to hunt both of them down. Scanning the crowds, a patch of red caught her attention, and she had her next target. Grady would have to wait until she dealt with the big red guy. She needed to know if the man was an actual threat or he if was just a horrible person. Did he treat all people who didn't donate the same way? Or was he undercover on a mission to stop her?

But that would mean her cover was blown.

She needed to catch him immediately.

Two streets flew by with the man in the red suit still in her eyesight. The gap between them lessened, and soon he was nearly in her grip.

"Stop, now!" Vera shouted in her most FBI authoritative voice. Her boots thwacked hard against the concrete sidewalk. "Get down!"

He continued three more steps, then his plastic boot hit black ice. Suddenly, the man was falling backward. His shocked face with its loose, tied-on beard looked into her eyes above him. The beard shifted, exposing his identity, and in a split second, she recognized one of Nico's goons.

Judging by the flash of evil in his eyes, he recognized her as well. That was why he tripped her.

Vera had no time to contemplate what was happening. She had no lead in this case, no intel to share with Tangen's team, and her cover was about to be blown. Her throat hitched, because she wanted to scream at how fast months of work would go down the drain. But she had no choice. She had to take this man out or he would destroy the case and her.

Blood rushed to her face as her protective mode took over. Her arms reached for the goon's neck before he hit the ground. Swinging him around, she brought her knee up into his nose. Gasps from the surrounding crowd followed the cringing crunch of contact. All they saw was this woman attacking Santa Claus.

But Vera saw the knife in his hand.

His right arm shot out, and the crowd shrieked, scattering all at once.

"Hello, Roxie," he said, but the tone of his voice was anything but pleasant. Blood filled his fake beard. "Boss is going to love when I take you in. And you don't have to be alive."

His empty hand reached out, aiming to grip Vera's throat, but he was too slow for her skill. Her top-notch FBI training had prepared her for every type of attack and from all directions. Vera dodged him, grabbing his knifed hand and, in one smooth motion, flipped him directly over her shoulder. Santa landed with a tremendous smack on the concrete. An expletive and a groan followed before he passed out.

The takedown was over as fast as it had begun. She would need Tangen's team here quickly for cleanup, but before she could make that call, she looked around at who had witnessed the scene. In all her undercover personas, she never felt so exposed. The street was mostly empty. People had run to their safe places. Vera figured most of them were calling the cops now. Maybe her cover could remain intact if she disappeared quickly.

She took her phone from her pocket and speed-dialed her handler. The phone rang and rang as Vera turned around to see if the van was nearby. She halted in mid turn. A growing rock in her stomach plummeted.

Two men with black curly hair stood on the opposite side of the street, a blue Porsche beside them. The older of the two pointed at the car. Even from this distance, she could see molten anger in his flashing blue topaz eyes.

"Get in," he instructed.

There was no question now for Vera. Her days as Roxie Moon were over. Her days as an FBI agent just might be as well.

"I can explain," Vera said, even though she wasn't

sure which excuse she would run with. Whichever one she chose wouldn't be the truth, and she knew Rafe would know.

"Get. In."

Vera pocketed the unanswered phone and pushed back her shoulders. She stepped Roxie's high-heeled boots down off the curb, and with every click and tap toward the Porsche, her brain configured her next move.

At the car door, Rafe opened it without a word.

"Would you believe me if I told you I took a self-defense class?" she asked.

His lack of laughter told her to keep trying.

She shouldn't be so shaken, but she'd never come this close to the edge of blowing her cover. She could assume her cover was gone and just refuse to go with them—or she could play this out until the end, keeping up with the mission until she was actually sure there was no resuscitating it back to life.

"You coming?" Grady asked from the other side of the car. Vera couldn't be sure, but she thought she saw sadness in his eyes. He trusted her, and she just proved to him he'd slipped up.

"Yeah." Vera nodded, preparing herself for the barrage of questions she knew both men would assault her with. It was a good thing her handler wasn't answering the phone. She would be fired on the spot.

☙

R‍AFE DROVE through the city and over the George Washington Bridge. Roxie, or whoever she was, sat beside him in the passenger seat while his son folded himself into the back jump seat that was barely a seat. Rafe wasn't sure where he was taking her, but he did know there was a sudden alteration to the new, fragile relationship he had with this woman.

He felt as though he'd been gutted.

It made no sense. He had just met the woman, but he went to bat for her. He told his best friend she could be trusted, that she wasn't a plant. She was worse than a plant.

She was a skilled *killer*.

If he hadn't seen how she took down that grown man with her own skinny hands, he would never have believed it. The man could be left for dead.

"Santa?" Rafe shouted the only word that would come out of his mouth.

She rolled her eyes at him. "Oh, please. You and I both know that was not Santa."

"Who are you? That's all I want to know." He

forced himself to ask this imperative question. He needed to know who he'd allowed to get too close to him.

"You can't know," she said, reaching for the handle.

He sped up. "No way. You're not going anywhere until you tell me the truth. Where did you learn…to do that? Back there. How?"

"I can't tell you. If I told you, then I'd have to kill you." She flashed him an irritating smile.

"Don't. Don't make light of this. Don't play innocent. That's unfair."

She gawked. "Unfair? What is this, first grade?"

"Roxie, you broke that man's nose. Just like you broke mine!"

"If I wanted your nose broken, it would've been broken."

Rafe hit the steering wheel. "Stop it! You know what I mean. Has everything you've said and done been planned and calculated?"

"Yes." She faced forward, her agitating smile gone.

"Even that song?"

Her lips trembled. "Not that. I'm still trying to figure that one out." She spoke the last part under her breath.

"Song?" Grady asked from the back.

Rafe looked in the rearview mirror. "Roxie, here, is an opera singer, as well as a killer. Fancy that."

She turned quickly his way. "I am not a killer, and I resent that."

"Then what are you and who are you? Answer the question!"

"That's technically two questions."

Rafe faked a laugh. "My bad. Two questions. Two very important questions that you have yet to shed some light on. What are you hiding?"

"I could ask you the same question."

"I'm not the one who just took down a man double your size."

"Are you mafia, Roxie?" Grady asked quietly.

"No." Her answer came swiftly.

"And you're not an assassin?"

"No."

At the next stoplight, Rafe faced Roxie fully. He couldn't figure her out. Did he trust a word that came out of her mouth? "I want to believe you. But it's too risky."

"So, what? You're just going to kill me? Make me disappear in the Hudson River?"

"What?" A chill ran up his spine as he gripped the steering wheel tightly. The metallic taste crept onto his tongue. He swallowed hard, fighting his rapid breathing. Now she was accusing him of being a killer? His throat burned, and when the light turned green, he didn't move. "I think you've got the wrong idea about me. Besides, you're the one with the gun. Not me. I'd much rather carry a knife."

"Dad?" The shock in Grady's voice had Rafe flooring the gas pedal and zipping up two blocks before saying anything else.

"So, he does call you Dad," Roxie said. "Sounds like the two of you are close, even with the adoption."

"That's none of your business." Rafe looked in the rearview mirror. "Watch it, Grady. There can be no slip-ups."

Rafe took the next left, downshifting with a trembling hand. He was terrified, and there was no hiding it. His core shook as his adrenaline pumped. Rossi could never find out about this. About Grady.

"You look like you're about to have a heart attack. Your face is covered in sweat." Roxie handed him a used napkin from his console.

He pushed it away. "Don't act like you care. You may be in the business of taking people out, but all I've ever wanted was to protect my son."

She dropped the napkin but not her gaze from him. "You mean that."

"Of course I do. I'm not the liar here."

"I'm not a liar either. But my job…my job calls for me to pretend so I can save lives."

"And what job is that?"

Roxie picked up her phone again. Her knee bounced nervously. She made a call, but when no one answered, she tossed the phone onto the console, appearing frustrated. "FBI. I'm an undercover agent. And I just blew my cover because my handler is not answering the phone!"

A low whistle emanated from Grady. "See, Rafe? I told you there was more to her."

"You got a badge?" Rafe asked.

She deadpanned. "No undercover agent carries their badge with them when they are undercover. That would be a death sentence."

Rafe reached for the phone. Surprisingly, she didn't stop him. He re-dialed the last number she had just called. Three rings passed before someone answered.

"BJ's Cleaners," the voice said on the other end.

"Liar," Rafe said. "Tell me who you really are."

"Who do you think I am?"

"I don't care. I just want you people to leave me

alone. That's all I've ever wanted. Just leave me alone." Rafe spoke into the phone, but his gaze leveled on Roxie.

The guy on the line replied, "We can't do that, Mr. Sinclair. Your restaurant has been tagged for a crime. Until I have another lead, you're my number one suspect. Please know that your car is being followed and anything that you do with my agent will be added to the list of charges, and you will never see the light of day again. Do we understand each other?"

Rafe swiped at his sweating forehead. "What… what crime are you talking about? Creare is clean. Every invoice, every payroll check, all of it. We have always been by the book."

"Then I guess you have nothing to worry about. Pull over and let my agent out."

Rafe glanced her way. "He wants me to let you out. Is that safe?" He looked in the rearview mirror at numerous cars and trucks lined up behind him. The man could be bluffing, or he could be right behind him.

But so could Rossi's men.

"Give me the phone." She held out her hand.

The phone practically slipped from his slick hand

into hers. He checked the mirrors again and then again for a third time.

"We can't go back," Roxie said to the man on the phone. "We've all been compromised. I made a promise to keep Grady safe." She locked her gaze on Rafe. "I mean to keep that promise."

Rafe could hear the man shout through the phone, and Rafe didn't need to know the exact words to know her handler was not happy with the direction of this conversation.

"I'll let you know where we are when we get there." She clicked off and pocketed the phone into her coat.

Rafe gawked at her, his jaw slack. "I don't understand."

She shrugged. "The FBI will say I've gone rogue."

"What does that mean? I mean, I know what it means, but what does it mean for you?"

"I suppose I most likely will be fired, but that's only if I survive. What it means for now is that we no longer have the protection of my team. But I agree with you in that if we stop this car, we most likely will be riddled with bullet holes. Keep driving and don't stop unless I am dead. Even then, don't stop." She reached the top of her head and pulled out some pins.

"What are you doing?"

She lifted the red hair straight off her head, revealing light blond hair in a bun. "If I have to die today, I will die as myself." In the next second, she stuck her finger in her eyes, one at a time, and flung two contacts to the floor. She reached down into her boot, lifting a 9 mm gun. Resting it on her thigh, she laid her head back but never closed her eyes. Her gaze watched the side mirror. "Head upstate."

"I took the wrong bridge for upstate New York. We're in New Jersey. It'll be a while to backtrack."

"That's good. If anyone's following us, maybe we'll lose them with the quick change in direction."

Rafe took another interstate route to make their way north. Glancing in the mirror, he didn't see another car make the switch behind them. "Are you able to tell me your name? Your real name?"

Her breathing sounded controlled, every inhale and exhale the same length. "Vera Sharp," she replied on the next exhale.

"You mean Special Agent Vera Sharp."

Her head tilted his way. "For now." She glanced back at the side mirror. "What were you going to do with me before you knew I was an agent?"

"Not dump you in the Hudson River like you thought."

Her cheek twitched. If she was trying to suppress a smile, she failed miserably. "You thought of something. Spill."

He shrugged. "I thought about putting you in my freezer. It's soundproof."

Vera burst out with a short laugh. "Oh, that's cold. Literally."

"I would have given you a coat and gloves. I'm not a monster."

"How nice of you."

Grady asked, "Why were you trailing me? What were you going to do with me?"

His son sounded sad, but he had trusted Roxie... *Vera* the most.

"So, you did see me. I figured so when you lost me. I was just going to make sure you were on the first plane out of here. I was going to send you home." She looked at both of them, first at Grady, then at him. "But the two of you had other plans. Care to share what you were up to?"

Grady replied, "The reason I came north from North Carolina was because my biological grandfather donated a large sum of money to my alma mater. It couldn't have been random, but was a message meant for me."

"This upset you? Most people would see that as a kind gesture. Maybe he was trying to make amends."

Rafe shook his head. "Nico Rossi does not make amends."

Vera's boxy breathing that had been controlled suddenly became erratic. Strong inhales flared her nostrils, and the whites of her eyes doubled in size.

"Vera? Say something." Rafe slowed the car. Was the woman having a heart attack? Something was physically happening to her.

"Vera!"

She raised a hand. "Just give me a minute to process this. How is Grady's grandfather Nico Rossi?"

"Well…" Rafe wasn't sure why this was so difficult to understand. "I had a relationship with his daughter."

Vera shook her head. "His daughter died in a car accident. I read the autopsy. It was twenty…"

"Twenty-five years ago," Rafe finished for her. "I know. I was there." It was all he could say. Rehashing that night took a lot out of him. He glanced in the mirror at Grady.

"My mom didn't want my grandfather raising me. She knew I would be corrupted. She and Rafe left the city before she gave birth. They found an older couple named Maribel and Todd Andrews, who agreed to raise me in the mountains of North Carolina. But we always knew it would only be a matter of time before Rossi found me."

"He'll kill you," Vera said matter-of-factly.

Rafe stared at her. "Yes, we know. But how do *you* know?"

"Rossi leaves no loose ends. My parents were loose ends."

Rafe lost the ability to inhale as he sought Vera's face for what she wasn't saying. "He…"

"Killed them, yes. Nico Rossi butchered my parents…in cold blood."

CHAPTER 5

"*I*t was fifteen years ago. I was a rookie cop in the Hamptons and wanting to see some action." Vera leaned her head back on the headrest as she pulled that life-changing night back to share. "I was shadowing a detective, drinking coffee late at night at a diner. Thankfully, insomnia was my first partner and never let me down."

The night she wished had never happened spilled from her lips...

VERA TOOK a deep sip and put the mug back onto the Formica counter, cringing at the day-old bitterness. Grabbing the sugar jar, she poured a generous amount of the sweet, white substance into the remaining sludge.

"When did you brew this?" Vera asked the lone waitress.

Detective Mike Shelby, who sat beside Vera, picked up his own mug and downed the contents. He sighed heavily. "Perfect. You need to get used to the late-night joe, Sharp. It comes with the job."

"I must've missed that in the job description." Vera glanced at her cup and shrugged. She downed the rest and mimicked Mike's sigh. Then coughed with a bit of a gag. She glanced at her watch. "What are we waiting for? Shouldn't we be out catching bad guys?"

"Enjoy the solitude. It can change in a split second."

"I think the traffic cops are seeing more action than we are."

"I can arrange for you to join them." Mike winked her way. The radio at his shoulder crackled, with the dispatcher's voice following. He listened, then lifted a hand to the waitress. "Can we grab two croissants to go?"

Vera jumped from her seat. "We're taking the call?"

"For you, anything. You want to see some action? Your wish is my command. Someone called in a break in. Let's go check it out and do some detecting." His gap-toothed smile made Vera like the man even more.

"Where to?" Vera grabbed the bag from the waitress and rolled up the brown paper. When Mike reached for it, she held it away and said, "For later."

"That doesn't seem fair. I'm getting off my butt for you." The bell jingled over the door as he held it for her. They walked to the unmarked car Mike used as a plainclothes detective.

Vera, however, wore her full blues. She had moved up from desk duty to shadowing the investigation unit. She believed being a detective was her future, and Mike was kind enough to let her tag along tonight.

He drove through the dimly lit streets, full of shadows and neighborhood secrets. The sizes of the homes grew and so did the acreage that belonged to them. He pulled up to a house with a black gate. The gate stood wide.

"Shall we go in?" He flashed her a smile. "Perhaps we'll catch them red-handed."

Vera grinned, unable to contain her excitement. This adrenaline rush propelled her to seek the profession. She had yet to cuff her first bad guy and could only hope her first arrest would be tonight.

Mike shook his head. "Don't get too excited, rookie. It most likely is the teenage son bringing a girl home with his parents out of town, setting off the alarm."

Vera had to figure Mike was right. Still, she readied her gun and proceeded with the correct protocol. Treat every call as the one that could go wrong.

At the door, Mike announced their presence, warning whoever was inside. When no response came, he nodded to

Vera to stand back. She shook her head, but he wasn't allowing her to go in.

Suddenly, the light inside turned on, but before Vera could step inside, Mike returned to stop her. He ushered her back to the car.

"What's going on?" she asked, trying to see over his shoulder.

"We need to stand down. Nothing going on here." He held the door for her, practically pushing her inside. His goofy grins were gone, replaced by a thin lip-line of worry. When they reached the end of the street, he shouted directions at her. "You were never here. You understand? You saw nothing."

"I didn't see anything!" Vera shouted back. "What happened?

Mike continued to look in the rearview mirror without saying a word. Halfway back to the police department, he asked, "Have you ever heard of Nico Rossi?"

Vera shrugged. "Sure. But I always thought he didn't really exist. He was like the bogeyman."

"He exists."

Vera glanced behind them. A car with its headlights tailed them. "We're being followed."

"I know. I'm going to have to pull over soon. I'll tell them you saw nothing. We were just in the wrong place at the wrong time."

"We were answering a call. That's what we're supposed to do." Vera noticed how Mike's hands trembled against the steering wheel.

"Nobody was supposed to get that call. I answered it for you not realizing..."

"Not realizing what?"

"The message was that it was a false alarm. But I still went over to check it out. Someone's dirty."

"You mean in the department?"

The lights flashed behind them. Whoever it was, chose a desolate road to come up alongside them and pull them over. Mike slowed the car and brought it to the curb. He put the car in park and rolled down the window.

"Don't look at anyone. Just face forward and stay low."

"I don't like this. It's not right."

"Well, if you live after tonight, you can make it your crusade to change the way of things. If it's all the same to you, I'm getting ready to retire and just want a little house on the beach."

Two men approached the car, one on either side. They were dressed in black with their coat collars pulled high and brimmed hats on their heads.

True to his word, Mike let the men know she saw nothing. But that also meant he was admitting to seeing whatever happened in the house. The men let them go.

The next day, Mike retired.

Two days later, his body was found by the shore, with a self-inflicted gunshot wound to his head.

"He didn't kill himself," Vera told anyone who would listen. "There's a dirty cop in the department." And then she dared to speak Rossi's name, and her crusade came to a brutal end.

"He killed your parents to show you his power," Rafe said after Vera grew quiet after sharing about that pivotal night in her life.

"They had come home from seeing a movie. It was approximately 9:30 p.m. on April 12. They had entered through the back kitchen door, and immediately my mother was struck but not killed. My father tried to fight back, so they killed him immediately, then returned to torture my mother before shooting her. There was no sign of a break-in. It was not only clean, but there was evidence planted that...that I did it."

Rafe glanced at the mirror to look at his son before glancing back at Vera. "You were framed for killing your parents?" he said, trying to wrap his mind around the statement.

"The night they stepped up to the car, they asked

for my cap. I gave it to the man without even thinking. They used a couple of strands of hair in the hat to leave at the scene."

"Were you arrested?"

"It was clear that if I didn't shut my mouth, I would be. And so..."

"And so you left the police department and joined the FBI."

"Bingo. It didn't take long to find someone else who had their own crusade against Rossi. Or I should say Tangen found me."

"Did you ever figure out who was the inside man?"

"Yes. Surprisingly, he used to be FBI until he took the bribe. In fact, he was my handler's old partner."

Rafe huffed a sick laugh. "Hence, the crusade. You lost your parents, and your handler lost his wingman."

"And you lost your son," Vera said in a near whisper.

Rafe glanced at Grady again. His son was alive and well, but Rafe understood what she meant. He lost raising his son. He lost the first steps, the firsts of everything else, as well as the seconds and thirds.

Rafe picked up his speed, passing Poughkeepsie to his left. He'd made this drive many times to visit his friends in the northwest corner of Connecticut and knew the back roads well. He thought about getting off the highway for the country route.

"Where are we going?" he asked his copilot. "Other than upstate, please."

"A destination point for when all goes wrong. A team will be there. I'm hoping to regroup with them. Maybe save my job. They'll take you and Grady into protective custody. You'll be safe."

Rafe hit the brakes, taking the next exit on screeching tires. *No way.*

"What are you doing?" Vera screeched just as loud as she grabbed the passenger handle. Grady had nothing to grab, and Rafe heard the *oof* sound when his son hit the side of the car.

Rafe glanced in his rearview mirror to see if he was all right and to see if anyone followed. Being daylight and lots of traffic, it would be hard to tell if a car meant harm until it was too late.

"I haven't spent the last twenty-five years watching my every move, choosing my every relationship with care and consideration, and keeping my distance from my son to have some unknown FBI agent and his team alert Rossi that Grady exists. It won't take the man long to do the math and figure out what happened to his long-lost grandson."

"Dad, I'm sure he already figured it out." Grady righted himself in the backseat, this time holding the two front seats for support. The old car had a lap belt in the back. Grady looked for the buckle and secured himself for the ride. "I wouldn't have risked coming to New York if I didn't think so. I've got my own problems I'm dealing with back home. This trip was the last thing I needed right now. I just knew I had to let you know about the donation as soon as I saw it."

"That was a risk all in itself," Rafe said. "What kind of problems are you having? And what if I was being watched?"

"You were," Vera said, looking at a map on her phone. "By me, and most likely Rossi's *and* Vargas's men."

Rafe wanted to know what Grady was struggling with, but Vera's comment stole his attention. "Gus? Are you saying my best friend is watching me? That's a lie."

"Got it," she said under her breath and pinned her location on her phone.

Throwing Gus under the bus was one strike against her. Giving up their coordinates to anyone and everyone made her the enemy or at least stupid. "Some undercover agent you are." Rafe rolled the window down halfway. He snatched the phone from Vera and threw it out into the woods along the roadside. "We're going dark."

The lethal glare she sent him made him remember what she did to the man dressed as Santa Claus. Stupid move or not, Rafe knew he wouldn't last three seconds in a ring with her.

"That was a secure line," she said. "The only two people with access were me and my handler."

"That makes it non-secure. I don't know your handler. I don't even know you. Maybe I should leave you on the side of the road, too." The thought took shape. It wasn't a bad idea.

"That would be signing your death certificate. Believe it or not, Mr. Sinclair, I'm the only friend you have. You may think you chose your friends wisely, but all you did was keep your enemies close. If Rossi knows about Grady, which I am sure he does, it's because of your so-called friend Gus. Now, where are you taking us? I need to figure out a safe place before you get us all killed."

Rafe bit the inside of his cheek to keep from accusing the woman of being all wrong. But he couldn't shake the fact that Gus was the only other person on this earth who knew Grady was Rossi's grandson. Still, she had to be wrong. Gus had earned his place of complete trust in Rafe's life. Gumbo wouldn't put Grady's life at risk for anything. He loved the boy as much as Rafe did. Sometimes Rafe thought he loved him even more, which was impossible.

Impossible, just like the story Vera was touting.

"Well? Where are we going?" Vera asked again.

"We're going to my friend's house. It's secluded, and I know for a fact that it is more secure than any location you have planned."

"Great. Another of your friends. Does he know about Grady?"

"*She*. And no, she doesn't. But it's time I tell her. Maybe if I had, things would have been different between us."

Vera huffed a laugh. "Ah, I see. One of your many girlfriends, huh? What number is she? Number 935? Or is it 1,935?" The snide comment told Rafe there was no point in denying the accusation. It wasn't an accusation if it was almost true. He let her exaggerate because he knew the list was endless, comical even. He'd painted himself as some sort of noncommittal womanizer. It was safer that way.

"I can never have a relationship without putting someone at risk." He drove to a fork in the road. One road led to remote isolation for hours. The fork to the right would take him to civilization and Mel's house. Check that. Mel and Jeremy Stiles's house. Mel and her *husband's* house. The number one couple in the world that turned Rafe's stomach green with jealousy. They had what he could never have, what he once dreamed of having when he was young and naïve and what he wished he could have with Mel when they worked together—even if he knew he would leave her within a few weeks like he did every other woman. He had to. He had no choice.

"You've dated an obscene amount of woman to keep them safe?" Vera wasn't buying his excuse. "Safe from whom? You?"

"Long-term dating is too risky for me. For Grady, and for the women," Rafe said as he took the familiar fork to the right, the proverbial road most traveled. He'd been down this road so many times, and it ended the same way all the time—with another parting fork—change his ways and put everyone at risk or accept his way of life and live alone. As much as he envied Mel and Jeremy and their life of love, visiting them reminded him of how relationships make people vulnerable. Everyone knew their weakest point—each other. Rafe could never put someone in the same life he had to live, always owing someone.

He drove through country roads of pristine pastures and acres of horse fences that surrounded unattainable fairytale lifestyles. "Dating may be dangerous, so I keep things short and sweet. I could choose to be a hermit and never talk to another woman, but I guess I don't like being alone. If you find fault with that, then so be it. If it makes me a jerk, then I guess I am. But at least I have a few weeks of feeling alive, and they're free to go on to be someone else's true love. Someone else's Achilles heel."

Vera was quiet as he pulled into Mel's driveway. Their storybook mansion loomed ahead, all wood and glass, yet a natural part of the forest backdrop. It produced the same jealous feeling as always.

"It's safe," Vera said, glancing up at the house.

"Yeah, no one will know we're here. And Jeremy's a cop."

"No. I meant love."

Rafe studied her profile until she turned his way and captured him with her intense blue eyes. He couldn't look away, no matter how much he tried. He knew Vera was strong but wondered if she knew her presence commanded just as much attention—

like when she sang on the stage and people poured in off the streets.

And when she brought him to tears.

"What about love?" he asked.

"It's safe. You don't have to be afraid of what it will do to you. Love will actually make you stronger, not weaker." Vera opened the door and climbed out. She walked to the side of the house, obviously inspecting the grounds for security.

"She ain't wrong," Grady said from the back.

Rafe shook his head. "What do you know? You've lived a sheltered life with Andrews."

"Because you loved me." Grady folded down the front passenger seat to climb out. "Your love for me made you strong. How else were you able to do all you have to keep me safe? Sorry, Rafe, but love doesn't make you weak. Love gives you the strength to be more for someone. It's not your weakest link."

๏

RAFE WAS right about the place. In fact, the home and surrounding landscape felt fortified, suggesting the owners were prepared for an army of bad guys to arrive at any moment. But who?

"What went down here?" Vera asked as she came

around the backside of the house. She approached Rafe and Grady at the bottom of the stone steps. "Either your friends are severely paranoid, or they're preparing for the end of the world. There are actually trenches in the woods. And I think I saw an entrance to a bunker."

Rafe shrugged. "Jeremy likes to build things in his spare time. Plus, Mel and Jeremy were nearly killed by a stalker a few years back. It happened here. You wouldn't know it now, but the house was destroyed. I guess Jeremy isn't ever letting anything like that happen again."

"Will he be okay with you hiding here?" Vera took the steps before the men and rang the doorbell. She then stepped down and waited at the bottom of the stairs for someone to answer.

"Hello?" a woman's voice came over the intercom.

"Mel? It's me, Rafe. Are you home?"

"Rafe? Sure! I'll be down in a minute. Just putting the baby down for a nap."

"Baby?" Vera angled an arched eyebrow at him. "You didn't mention a baby."

"I forgot."

"You forgot your friends had a baby? What kind of friend does that?" Vera caught Rafe quickly glance at Grady before moving up the steps. She bit her tongue, wishing she could take back those words. They had been insensitive. Perhaps Rafe struggled with seeing his friends live the family life he never could. "I'm sorry. I guess I see how the two of you have found a way to have a relationship, even if it doesn't look like what others view as normal. But just so you know, family looks different for everyone. And family isn't about blood."

The door swung wide, and in the next second, a woman in her mid-thirties with brown curly hair and brown eyes squealed in delight and lurched herself into Rafe's arms. He lifted her off the ground, and it was obvious the two of them were close—or had been at one time. As Rafe brought her feet back to the landing, Vera recognized the woman from one of the photos in his office. It was the photo where he had his arms around two women.

But Mel was the woman Rafe looked at with puppy-dog eyes.

Vera thought Mel was pretty, even if her hair wasn't long like in the picture and was now a bit frizzy.

Vera choked out a cough, clearing her throat to smother it. Where had that thought come from? It didn't feel professional but rather judgmental. It sure didn't meet her job's requirement of collecting intel, but instead felt...personal.

Was she jealous of this woman? *Why?*

Suddenly, Mel reached to her to shake hands. "Who is this, Rafe?" Mel elbowed him in the ribs. "Introduce me to your...friend."

Did she think there was something romantic between them? Vera had to put an end to that idea immediately.

She didn't take Mel's hand. "I'm Special Agent Vera Sharp. Rafe is under investigation. We need your home for a secure location while we wait for our next orders."

Mel's hand dropped as her face blanched. "Rafe? What is she talking about? Is this true? Are you in trouble?"

"No. Vera has a flare for the dramatic. She should save that for the stage." Rafe said the last part through clenched teeth aimed at her. "For someone who can put a crowd at ease with a song, you sure lack finesse in the conversation department."

"I state the facts, Mr. Sinclair." There, that'll put the professional distance back between them, she thought.

"The jury's still out on those facts." To Mel, Rafe

asked, "May we come in? We'll explain everything to you. I promise."

Mel rubbed her palms on her jeans and pulled her blue cardigan sweater tight around her. "Um... okay. But I need to call Jeremy and have him come home from work. He'll want to be here for this." She turned to enter the house.

"That's a good idea." Rafe put his hand on Mel's back. So comfortably, Vera thought without being able to stop the response from surfacing.

Vera stood back to regroup from the way her mind was reacting. Grady followed Rafe and Mel inside, but he stopped at the threshold to let her pass first. "You have nothing to worry about," he whispered.

Vera felt her mouth fall open. She was ready to deny such a statement, but no words came out. She straightened her shoulders and brushed past Grady. "Well, someone needs to worry. A lot of people are going to die in a couple of weeks if I don't. If that's what you meant."

Grady frowned and whispered, "No, it's not, but now that you mention it, I am worried about the same thing back home."

Vera stopped cold. "Rossi?"

Grady shook his head. "There are more bad guys

in this world than can be caught. I'm beginning to think most never are."

Vera squeezed Grady's hand. "We still never stop trying. Ever."

He nodded and squeezed back.

"If you want to talk about it, let me know. I can contact the North Carolina office and have an agent sniff around."

"I'd be afraid of what they would find and who would be involved."

Vera looked at Rafe standing off in the kitchen. He leaned against the granite countertop with his arms folded as Mel made the phone call. He appeared relaxed, even under the circumstances.

"Are you trying to protect someone?" Vera asked. How far would Grady go to protect someone he loved, even if that someone meant harm?

Including his own father.

"I'm trying to protect my town from those who want to ruin it. I didn't tell Dad yet, but I moved to the coast. Royal Bay is my home now."

Home.

Vera wasn't sure where her home was anymore. One undercover persona to the next; one town to another. Could she relate to Grady's dilemma when her home changed with the seasons? She hadn't stepped foot in the home her parents were killed in since their deaths. She'd allowed Rossi to steal that from her too without even realizing it.

"Don't let them take it, Grady. Be vigilant, or it will happen in the blink of an eye. Trust me."

Grady offered a sad smile. "I do, Vera. I trust you. With everything." He smiled and jutted his head toward Rafe. "Even if he doesn't."

Mel ended the phone call. "Jeremy's on his way," she announced, walking up to Grady, who now stood in front of an enormous fireplace hearth. The exposed stone chimney reached to the open second floor. The home felt like stepping into a magazine. But as beautiful as every corner was, the place didn't feel untouchable. In fact, Grady reached for a small wooden angel on the shelf, and Mel didn't stop him.

"Jeremy made that for me when we were kids," she said with pride in her voice. "He carves the most amazing things. He made our kitchen table, too. But that's a whole other story. For now, I'd love to know who you are. Are you an agent as well?"

Grady put the angel down. He shoved his hands into his coat pockets, a sheepish grin on his youthful face. "No, ma'am. I'm studying to be a chef...like my dad."

Rafe stepped up to stand beside Grady. "Mel, this

is Grady." After a deep sigh, he said, "He's my son. He was given up for adoption as a baby."

The warm home stilled for about ten seconds, and Vera wondered if the atmosphere would remain inviting. It appeared everyone waited for Mel's direction.

"Oh, Rafe. I had no idea. I wish I had—"

"No. You couldn't. No one could."

Mel nodded, but confusion spread across her face. She then reached out her arms for Grady. "I don't understand, but I'll just start loving on you right now anyway, if that's okay with you."

"It's fine with me," Grady said with a beaming smile.

As Mel hugged Grady tight, Vera watched a tear slip from the corner of Rafe's eye. He brushed it away quickly, but when he noticed she saw, he mumbled, "You didn't see that."

Vera pressed a smile away to keep a serious composure. "Mr. Sinclair, it's my job to notice everything."

"I'm counting on you to do just that. And it's Rafe."

CHAPTER 6

*R*afe searched through the cabinets to take stock of potential dinner ingredients. The pickings were sparse unless he could create an oat cereal and mashed peas concoction. He supposed he'd been presented with worse during his training. Some of those instructors at the Institute took delight in making the students squirm under the stress to excel.

"Maybe we should order out for pizza," Mel suggested, bouncing her baby boy on her hip. Little Joey, named for Mel's father who lived nearby with his wife Arlene, had just passed his eighth-month mark. He lifted his little head and looked at Rafe before hiding his face in the crook of Mel's neck.

"He's afraid of me." Rafe closed one cabinet and opened another.

"No, he's just playing shy with you. He'll get used to you…soon."

Rafe ignored the hint of a question in her voice about how long he would be at their home. He wanted that answer, too. He picked up a container of breadcrumbs and sighed. "Pizza takeout instead of mashed peas? Have you forgotten my skill with unique ingredients? I'm hurt."

"I'm just as bummed not to have you cook for us tonight. What a treat that would have been. I'll go shopping tomorrow or send Jeremy out with a list. I'm sorry, I haven't been able to get out more. Joey's a little temperamental out of the house."

The baby whined on cue.

"Shhh." Mel bounced faster. "It's okay, sweetie. Are you hungry?" She stepped up beside Rafe. "Grab me the peas. Here, hold him while I warm them up."

"I don't think that's a good idea. It's been years since I've held a baby. Twenty-five to be exact. I can warm the peas up. I'm fairly sure I can handle that."

"You don't know the temperature. It has to be perfect. Just take Joey, please."

Rafe exchanged the small jar for the wiggling baby, holding the boy at arm's length. They looked to size each other up. Rafe forced a smile. Joey frowned and let out a wail.

"See, I don't know what I'm doing."

Mel worked at the counter, scooping out the green mush. "You're not going to break him. Bring him closer and actually hold him."

Slowly, Rafe did as she instructed. He began to bounce like she had, and suddenly little Joey smiled.

"He likes that," Rafe said. He moved around the kitchen, bouncing and dancing a bit. He backed up, but when he turned around, his head met the cabinet door that was left open. "Ow!"

Instantly, Joey erupted into a fit of giggles. He pointed to the cabinet, his laughter growing louder.

Rafe rubbed his head to make the pain go away. "You found that funny, did you?" He shut the door to keep from hitting it again. Although, if that's what it took to make the boy stop crying, Rafe would consider another go at it.

"All ready," Mel said, reaching for her son. Suddenly, Rafe found his arms empty and joined her at the table. She put Joey in his highchair and prepared his bib and spoon for dinner. Soon, the green mush covered the boy's face, but he kept diving back for more.

"He likes that, too."

"It doesn't take much to make babies happy." Mel scooped him another spoonful. "Can you tell me a little about Grady? I mean, if you're comfortable. I can't believe you're a father."

"Not much to tell. Back when I was twenty, I dated Nico Rossi's daughter. Angela and I were going to run away together. I know, delusional, but we were young and naïve. But when she became pregnant, we had no choice. She said she couldn't tell her father. He would kill them, and I'm sure he would have, at least me anyway. My friend Gus arranged for us to stay at one of his family's rental properties down in North Carolina, and for nine months, we thought everything would be fine. Even after Angela had the baby. Then one night, we were driving home from the restaurant we worked at and were hit by a drunk driver. Angela was really hurt. Grady was with an older couple who watched him when we worked. Her dying words were to hide Grady. She died thinking her father found us."

"And you don't think he had? What happened to the driver?"

"As far as I know, he was arrested. I arranged for Grady to be adopted, and I returned to New York to start school. Gus's dad was putting me through the Institute, giving me a fresh start."

"Hmmm."

"What? You've got your thinking look on."

Mel shrugged. "That just sounds way too convenient. I know Gus is a good friend of yours, and he probably was only thinking of you, but it just seems odd for him to do all that out of kindness."

"Now you sound like Vera."

"Ah, so she questions his motives, too."

"Motives? Now you're making him sound like some sort of criminal."

"I'm sorry. That wasn't my intent. I'm just worried about you. For the FBI to be investigating you and the restaurant concerns me. Why would Nico Rossi think Creare is available to be part of his next heist? What gave him that idea? Who gave him that access? Is there something you're not telling us? How is he planning on using Creare?"

Rafe tunneled his fingers through his hair. He dropped into the seat beside her and folded his hands on the wooden table. "I wish I knew. I called Monroe to tell him to close for two weeks." He dropped his forehead into his hands. "I may never reopen. I was already hanging by a thread, depending on the Christmas season to push me back into the black. This couldn't come at a worse time."

Joey pushed the spoon away, signaling that he

was finished. Mel stood to clean him up. "It almost sounds like this was planned. Everything is too convenient for someone to come in and take over. Also, don't forget when I owned the restaurant, we had to shut down for a while, and you brought the place back. I have confidence that you'll do it again."

Mel reached and tussled his curls with a smirk on her sweet face. She brought the spoon and jar to the sink.

"Thank you, Mel. That means everything to me. Really. I want you to know I've always considered you a friend."

She turned back to face him. "And Chris and I have always considered you a friend. Speaking of which, we should call her. Not sure if you know that her husband Marcus isn't just an attorney in Savannah. He also has a coalition against organized crime. He may know things that we don't. He'll know what to look for, anyway. It wouldn't hurt to talk to him. May I call him?"

Rafe tapped the table. "Why not? What could it hurt? Everyone else is involved, including the FBI."

Mel shook her head. "I can't believe the FBI is investigating you. What did Agent Sharp say about all your girlfriends?"

"Let's just say she made her displeasure about them obvious."

"Interesting. She's pretty. And you say she sings, too?" Mel picked up a sleepy Joey and cradled him in her arms. She swayed back and forth, and soon the boy's eyes drifted closed. Motherhood looked good on her. It softened her where she had once been so hard and angry with the world. Mel would say her faith in God changed her, but Rafe believed she was always there under the surface, just waiting to bloom.

"Like a songbird," he replied to her question. "Vera has a voice like I've never heard before. How she ended up in law enforcement boggles my mind. But everyone has their reasons for their choices, and hers are valid."

"And you have a valid reason for yours. I see that now more than ever." She kissed her baby's forehead, then whispered, "I'm going to go put him to bed."

Rafe stood and headed to the back kitchen door. He looked out into the forest that went for miles. "I think Vera and Jeremy are still out in the backwoods. He's giving her the full tour. I think I'll go find them. Or at least find Grady. He's around here somewhere."

"I like him. He's a kind young man. I hope

someday the two of you can have a full relationship with no fear or risk. That's what I'm going to pray for."

"I'm not much of a praying man, never felt worthy. But I do appreciate you taking the time to bring that request to God." Rafe stepped outside and walked in the direction he had seen Vera and Jeremy go. He reached the tree line and peered through the thick forest. Glancing back at the house, he wondered where Grady went. The boy seemed worried about something back home on top of everything else going on. Rafe made a mental note to ask him about it later.

Turning back to the trees, he stepped into the forest to track down Vera. She needed to keep him in the loop of what her next plans were. She may be the agent in charge of the investigation, but he had the most to lose if all her plans failed. Treating him like a suspect needed to stop.

At dusk, the woods held shadowy places at every turn. As a city boy, getting lost in them was a solid possibility. Rafe had no desire to need a search and rescue team to come find him.

"Vera? Jeremy?" he called into the thick of it. A slew of birds flapped their wings and shook the leaves above him in response. He also didn't need to wake the forest and all its inhabitants—whatever kinds of animals that included. "Vera," he harshly whispered, not disguising the annoyance in his voice. "Where are you? I won't let you keep me out."

Rafe might not carry a badge, but he'd earned his place at the table. He'd dealt with Nico Rossi a lot longer than she had. And if anyone had a vendetta against the man, it would be him. Rafe needed to make sure he never learned about Grady. Were his days of protecting him ending?

Rafe had no idea what his son was getting into. Maybe the boy had been sheltered too much. In Rafe's plight to protect him from the evils of the world, he may have only set him up to be vulnerable and taken advantage of.

But at least he's not part of the mob, Rafe reasoned. As Rossi's sole male heir, Grady would have been positioned to take over the whole syndicate. Rafe didn't want to imagine who his son would be today if Rossi had raised him.

At least he has a fighting chance. Rafe could only hope.

He came to a fallen log. This was as far as he wanted to go in the forest. He took a left and walked parallel to the house. Golden lights from the windows guided him as the sun completely disappeared from the sky and dusk turned to dark.

Rafe had yet to see any sign that the two of them were out here. If he hadn't watched them step into the woods, he would say they were nowhere nearby. It was like they disappeared or were hiding from him.

Maybe they were.

Suddenly, Rafe remembered Vera mentioning something about a bunker. He wouldn't put it past Jeremy to build one. The man was retired Army and now law enforcement. With the brush with death, he and Mel had experienced, a bunker would be right up his alley.

Rafe made his way back closer to the house. It couldn't have been too far into the woods if Vera had seen it. Picking up his steps, he followed the tree line further to the left.

He heard voices before he saw anything out of the ordinary. He stopped cold and turned an ear to the sound.

The deep rumble of Jeremy's voice floated his way. Something about making a phone call at the police department. A scan of the forest before Rafe showed no sign of anyone.

"I've waited too long to inform my handler."

Vera's muffled voice carried his way. "I won't jeopardize this location, so I'll take you up on the offer to make the call at the department in town."

Rafe fisted his hands, unnerved at Vera's willingness to put them all at risk. Maybe he should have opened the car door and let her out. Bringing her here had been a big mistake. And since she planned to continue with her allegiance to this unknown handler, Rafe needed to get Grady out of here.

He turned left to exit the woods, but two steps later, he felt himself falling through the ground. It was as though the earth had just disappeared and all Rafe could do was let out a scream as he fell to his backside and slid down into the darkness.

"DID YOU HEAR SOMETHING?" Vera asked Jeremy. She stood from the table and chairs set up in a small underground bunker. The place was equipped with two rooms and a half washroom. It would keep a few people safe for a short amount of time. Jeremy estimated there were enough dehydrated food packets for four people to last a month, more if rationed. The retired army captain turned cop had thought of everything to survive. Vera just wasn't sure what made the Stiles family build it. What did they fear would happen? It seemed excessive.

Except here she was, arranging for Rafe and Grady to occupy the safe space until she could return for them. When she left Connecticut for New York City, she needed to know no one could find or touch them. Vera would be going under again, but not underground like them. It wouldn't be Roxie Moon making a comeback, though. That identity would be too dangerous. Rossi would be looking for her after she knocked out one of his men. This time, Winifred Winterbottom would be coming to the city to check up on her investment.

Creare.

"I'm not sure, but it might've been a bobcat letting out a cry. The sun just went down." Jeremy approached the opened door that led to a stairway. He peered up and around and shrugged at her. He still wore his officer's uniform and removed the flashlight from his belt. Flicking it on, he surveyed the area in the stairwell and above. "I don't see anything."

Vera followed him outside, shutting the lights off and closing the door behind her. "We should head back, anyway. We have a lot to discuss with Rafe and Grady. It's going to take some convincing to get them to be willing to call this place home for a few weeks. At least through New Year's. If I can intercept the explosives, then sooner."

"No offense, but I don't see Rafe agreeing to your plan." Jeremy locked the door and led the way up the stairs with the flashlight.

"You got that right!" Rafe's voice echoed all around them.

"Rafe?" Jeremy called, moving in a circle. "Where are you?"

"I'm in a hole. Get me out of here!"

"Keep talking so I can find you."

"That's fine with me. Because I have a lot to say. Especially to you, Vera. You may be in charge of your investigation, but you are not in charge of me. The only place I will ever call home is New York City. And I'm sorry about your parents, but right now, I have the most to lose. I will not sit by and hope for the best. I have never done that, and I'm not gonna start now."

Jeremy shined his flashlight down into a circular tunnel. The light reflected off Rafe's upturned face about 4 feet down. It was dark, and the man was covered in dirt, but there was no mistaking his anger.

"What happened?" Vera asked.

"What does it look like? I fell into a hole. Jeremy, what is this place?"

"It's a trap. I have a few of them around the woods. I have markers on the trees to tell me where they are."

"Traps, bunkers, trenches. What are you planning for?" Vera asked.

Jeremy moved the light onto her. "I'm planning to never be on the losing end of a fight again. I was left for dead in these woods. Never again."

Vera thought of Grady's words to her when they arrived at the house. There really were too many bad guys for one person to catch them all.

She looked down into the hole and couldn't believe she was contemplating bringing Rafe under-cover with her. But if he really was the fall guy, then he would need her before Rossi really buried him alive.

Kneeling at the edge, she reached a hand down into the ground. Rafe latched on with a tight grip. She said, "We do this your way, but with my plan. Understood?"

"And no one else," he said. "Forget about your handler. Forget about anyone else. I trust no one."

"But do you trust me?"

They locked gazes by the light of Jeremy's beam.

"I trust the woman I heard and saw on the stage. She was genuine. She was real."

"I was acting."

"You can keep lying to yourself, but that's the only time I ever saw who you truly are." He pulled up onto her arm as she braced her legs. As his upper arms surfaced, Jeremy pulled him the rest of the way up. They stood less than a foot away from each other, and it felt as though Rafe dared her to deny his words.

"It was just a song."

"And I'm just a cook."

Jeremy laughed and patted Rafe on the back. "A little humility might be a better tactic. Let's get back to the house. The two of you can work out the particulars on your own. But we do need to decide what to do with Grady."

"Protect him," Vera said at the same time as Rafe. "At least we can agree on that. But do me a favor, Chef Sinclair. Remember your domain is the kitchen. Mine is putting people in handcuffs or in the hospital. Don't get in my way."

Jeremy laughed again, walking up between them. He draped an arm around both of them. "On second thought, Rafe, you may have met your match. She's just as boastful as you are."

"It's not boasting if it's true," Vera said.

"Exactly," Rafe agreed.

Jeremy sighed. "Why do I bother? Okay, fine, have it your way. You both are the best. Now prove it."

Jeremy moved off in front, leaving them to walk back alone. They exited the forest and arrived back at the house just as a car pulled out of the driveway.

"It must be the pizza delivery," Rafe said.

"Great. We're just in time for dinner," Vera said. She held the kitchen door open for Rafe, noticing how filthy he was now that he stood in the light. "You might want to shower first."

"And let Grady can eat all the pizza? No way. I'll get my slices first."

"So, I shouldn't wait?"

"Not unless you want to go to bed hungry."

They entered the kitchen to find Mel looking worried. "Are the pizzas on the back steps?"

Vera shook her head. "No. They're not here? We just saw the car leave."

Jeremy walked to the front door and opened it. There was no sign of pizza boxes anywhere. "Maybe Grady already got them?"

Mel chimed in. "I ordered six pizzas. He wouldn't take all of them, would he?"

Rafe shook his head. "I was only kidding about that. Where is he?"

Mel replied, "I haven't seen him since before I put Joey in his crib. Grady said he was going to lie down, too. That you all have been up all night. But he's not in the room I gave him. I just checked."

Rafe ran through the kitchen and into the living room. He raced up the stairs, calling, "Grady!"

Vera couldn't wait to make her call. "We've been compromised," she said to Jeremy. "The car was a black SUV. I'll take your phone to make my call to my team. You put out an APB." Jeremy passed her his cell phone while he radioed the dispatcher at his department. He put out an all-points bulletin on Grady, relying on his wife's description of him.

"He looks just like Rafe," Mel said. "How did this happen? Are you sure he was taken? Maybe he went for a walk."

Vera dialed Tangen's direct line. After four rings, it went to voicemail. She wasn't expecting him to answer a strange number, but if he had also been compromised, she also couldn't connect them. She would need to go undercover again and would need her anonymity. As soon as the message beeped, Vera spoke in her crackly, aged persona.

"Hello there, laddie. Grammy is coming to town

and would love to see you. Hugs and kisses! See you soon, my dear." She clicked off just as car lights shone through the living room windows. The beams moved slowly as the car came to a stop out front.

Jeremy pointed at his wife. "Bedroom, Mel. Now. Lock the door." Mel followed directions without complaint. Jeremy removed his gun, as Vera did the same.

Vera shut off the lights and took the wall by the front door. She nodded to Jeremy that she was ready.

But ready for what? An ambush? Could she and Jeremy stop all of Rossi's goons with their single handguns? Rafe may have thought coming here was secure, but all he did was put this young family in harm's way.

And where was Rafe? What did he find upstairs? Was Grady up there? Is he alive? Perhaps Rossi's men were already in the house.

Vera watched Jeremy inch closer to the door-knob, his gun held at the ready.

"I'm so sorry," she whispered.

Jeremy nodded, his face stoic. "I'm ready this time," he whispered back, and Vera had to believe him. The man had equipped his home and land for any type of intrusion. If she had to be without her team, this would be the place she would want to be.

The sound of a car door opening and slamming followed by light footsteps up the path gave them warning of at least one person approaching. She could handle one, but Rossi wouldn't send just one.

"It's not him," she said.

Jeremy backed up to glance out the window through the edge of the curtain. His gun dropped. "Stand down. But be ready for anything. It looks like it's just the pizza."

He opened the door slowly with his gun down by his side. He inserted it into the back waistband of his pants. "Hey, Liam. Let me help you with that. Do we owe you anything?"

The voice of a young teenager spoke. "No, Mel paid for it already. Enjoy your night, Officer Stiles."

The boy's steps retreated to the car, and soon he was gone.

Jeremy closed the door, leaning back against it. He dropped the pizzas to the floor and slowly slid down the door until he also sat quietly. The sound of his deep breathing told Vera he needed a moment.

"I'm going to check on Rafe. Don't get too relaxed." Vera wanted to be sympathetic to Jeremy's trauma, but she needed him to stay with it. Until they found Grady, they weren't out of the woods yet.

"I'm fine. Just need a minute."

Vera could respect that. She took the stairs, light-footed and with her gun still held high. At the top, she went left toward Grady's room. The door stood wide, but she saw no sign of anyone. Inside, the room appeared untouched, just as Mel had said. Returning to the hall, Vera checked two more rooms. One of them was hers, but those also were empty. The only other room left was the loft above the garage.

Vera made her way to the other side of the home and found the door open. She stepped in sideways, halting at the sight of Rafe standing at an open window. He had his back to her as he stared out into the darkness. A white curtain billowed around him. The room was set up with a pool table and other games, but nothing felt fun at the moment.

"He's gone," Rafe said quietly. Without turning, he lifted his hand to reveal a balled-up piece of paper.

Vera stepped forward to retrieve it. Returning her gun to her boot, she used her shirtsleeve to hold the paper. It could be evidence of a crime. Carefully opening it to not leave her fingerprints, she could see it was a note.

Dad,

I have to go. You have sacrificed so much to protect me, but it ends here. It's time for me to grow up and stand on my own. Don't contact me, and I won't contact you again either. But know I love you and always will.

Grady

VERA BROUGHT the paper to a table. "It could be forged or forced."

"It's his writing. He left willingly. I knew something was up." Rafe leaned forward, resting his hands on the windowsill. "Now he's out there alone, and Rossi will grab him in a heartbeat."

"Or he's going after Rossi himself."

Rafe turned quickly. His eyes widened in unabashed fear. "He wouldn't last two seconds. Would he really do that? No. He wouldn't be that stupid."

Vera let it go. "Okay. You know your son better than I do," she said aloud. But in her mind, she thought, *only one way to find out. I'll need to find a car. Something a rich old lady would drive.*

Winifred Winterbottom would be paying Nico Rossi a visit.

CHAPTER 7

"I can't wait to see what Vera looks like," Mel said, pushing Joey in an infant swing from the big oak tree in the middle of the yard. She'd bundled the boy up for the chilly December air, but his cheeks were still bright red.

Rafe smiled at the boy, thinking of his own son out there somewhere. It had been two days since Grady left, and now that Vera had an older model Mercedes to use, it was time for her and Rafe to leave, too.

The car had been located by Jeremy's father, belonging to his neighbor, who agreed to lend it to Vera for a couple of weeks. With the car secured and Vera's disguise ready, it was time for them to head back to the city, just in time for the hustle and bustle of the holiday season.

Christmas was still a week away, which gave them two weeks to thwart the New Year's Eve heist. Vera was still no closer to figuring out the location or how they planned to pull it off, but she hoped her Mrs. Winnie persona could infiltrate the plan with her spry and unsuspecting investigative skills. When Rafe asked how she planned to do that, Vera reminded him to stick to the kitchen where he excelled and let her do her job.

"She is interesting, isn't she?" Rafe asked. "I don't think I've ever met anyone like her. I wish you could've seen her sing on Creare's stage. Or take down Santa. I still can't believe the same woman did both. It's hard to wrap my head around. The two don't go together, and yet when Vera is just Vera, she's both of them. Tough and charming."

Mel paused from pushing the baby swing. Her gloved hand held the swing still as her mouth dropped open. "I don't believe it."

"What? What don't you believe?"

"You like her."

"Well, sure. She's—wait. Let me get something straight. If you mean like her as in *like* her in a romantic way, no. That's impossible. She's not my type. She's way too serious and, honestly, a little scary."

"Too career driven for you, Rafe? You're used to picking women with no real plan to succeed. I think successful women scare you more because they might expect something from you. Admit it."

"Sure, fine, I admit it. It keeps the dating simple. But that's my point. I can't be interested in Vera Sharp. She doesn't fit into my lifestyle."

"But your choice in lifestyle doesn't have to continue. Don't make Grady's gift be in vain. He wants you to live and live fully."

"I have everything I need to be happy. I have my restaurant and food. I have friends, like you and Chris and Gus. And whether he wants to be part of my life or not, I will always have Grady, even if it's only in here." Rafe touched his chest over his heart. "I'm used to loving him from afar."

"But what if you had someone to share it all with on a daily basis? What if you had someone to do life with? Someone to love up close?"

"I don't really see an FBI agent excited about the culinary world. She doesn't fit. End of conversation."

Mel shrugged and scooped up her baby out of the swing. "If you say so. I'll let it go. But I am going to pray for you."

"I don't need your prayers. I've gotten by on my own for forty-five years. A prayer won't change anything that I couldn't do myself." He fell into step beside her as they headed back to the house.

"God does expect us to do what we can. But there comes a point where we've done all we can and have to trust Him to do what we can't. Have you done everything you can to save Creare?"

"Absolutely. But it's still failing. If I have to close the doors, I'll have no one to blame but myself. I don't want to rely on anyone to help me. I took money from Gus to buy your share. He said it was a gift, but I never felt right about it. I would just end up blaming others when everything falls apart."

"Because in your experience, everything always does."

"Yes. Exactly. Everything always falls apart. Everyone always leaves. If I don't depend on anything or anyone to begin with, then I'm no worse for the wear. I'll just pick up my knife and move on to the next restaurant."

Mel stopped and faced him. As she frowned, Joey touched her face, appearing to also sense his mother's sadness. "I'm so sorry. We left you, too. Chris and I."

Rafe held up both his hands to stop her. "Don't

go there. You and Chris have what I could only dream of."

"See? You *do* dream it. You just admitted to it."

"Dreaming is fine if you don't get stuck in the dream and stop living. I refuse to get stuck there. When life comes too close to the dream, I move on. It's safer that way."

"Because you believe the dream will never actually happen for you."

"My own son has told me not to contact him again. It's not a false belief when life at every turn has proven it to be true."

They approached the house the rest of the way in silence. He appreciated Mel wanted to help, but he'd been down this road enough times to know how his life would go. Inside the front door, two older women stood by the hearth. They looked to be in their seventies or even eighties. Rafe recognized one of them is Mel's mother, Arlene. She was fixing the white hair of the other woman.

"There, that's perfect. We could be twins, if not for the age difference." Arlene giggled.

"Aw, Arlene, I would love to be your honorary sister," the woman said in a crackly voice. She leaned in to kiss Arlene on the cheek. "Thank you for your help. You are a lovely lady."

Mel stepped up to the women. "I don't believe it. You fooled me."

Rafe wondered what the women were talking about. He also wanted to get going so he would arrive back in the city before five o'clock. "Anyone see Vera?"

Mel and Arlene erupted into laughter. The unknown woman walked up to him, moving slowly but still with a spring in her step for her age. She put out her wrinkled hand. Her fingers curled a bit from arthritis and there was a tremble in her grip, but he sensed some strength in her.

"Nice to meet you, Mr. Sinclair." Her deep voice also had a catch in it. "I'm Winnifred Winterbottom. From Greenwich, Connecticut. I would like to invest in your company."

"You would?" Rafe glanced over at Mel. Her face was beet red, and she looked like she was about to burst out laughing. "What's so funny?"

"She fooled you. You're right. She belongs on the stage. Sing for us, Winnie."

The woman opened her deep red lips and sang the first lines of the *Madame Butterfly* aria, the same one that Vera had sang. Only their voices sounded completely different. This woman's was a whole octave lower.

"Winnie? *Vera?*" Rafe peered into a set of blue eyes. Definitely Vera.

"I didn't have time to change the eye color. But that's okay, because Nico knows me as Roxie Moon with amber eyes. Blue eyes will be fine. But the rest of me is completely covered.

All Rafe could do was stare at every inch of her, from the white hair roots that looked so real to her laugh lines around her eyes and mouth to her pure white pantsuit that made her look like a million bucks.

"Nice duds," he said.

"They're Arlene's."

Arlene timidly said, "It's what I wore for Mel's wedding as the mother of the bride. I spared no expense."

Vera looked back at the woman. "I appreciate you giving this to me. And I promise to do my best to not to get blood on it."

Arlene laughed and then frowned. She didn't look like she was sure if Vera was joking or not. Rafe didn't have the heart to tell her that Vera was serious. Rafe didn't know Arlene too well, but knew she was diagnosed with schizophrenia and experienced emotional episodes that could be scary for someone who didn't know how to react or handle them. He didn't want to be the one to set one of those events off, although Arlene looked better every time he saw her.

"Are you ready to go?" Vera asked. "You can be my chauffeur."

Jeremy stepped up with a black suit and black cap. "Your costume."

Rafe put up his hand. "You never mentioned this. Why can't I drive my own car?"

Vera pursed her wrinkly lips. "Because they will be looking for a blue vintage Porsche. Jeremy's dad is going to put it in his garage for safekeeping. Don't worry. Nothing will happen to your car. Now go get dressed. I have a party to crash and can't be late."

Rafe grumbled, ripping the suit from Jeremy's hands. "Why couldn't I have been some rich investor like you? Why do I have to be a chauffeur? Or how about your personal chef who travels with you? That would make sense."

"You're wasting time, Jeeves," Vera said with a taunting smirk.

"Please don't tell me you're going to sit in the backseat the whole time like some *Driving Miss Daisy* movie."

"Of course. If I didn't, we would blow our cover in an instant. Once you put that suit on, you are no longer Rafe. Forget he exists. Think, feel, breathe, and act like a chauffeur. You will hold doors for me both at the car and in the buildings I enter. You will be a fly on the wall with your hands folded while you wait for me to return to the entrance. All the while, you will be listening to every conversation and watching every person who interacts. You will be my intel collector to tell me if something is going wrong. You will wear an earpiece connected to me. Thanks to Jeremy, I have a full setup. It's not state-of-the-art, but it will do."

"It looks like you've thought of everything. But can I pick a different name?"

"Absolutely. Who would you like to be?"

Rafe thought for a moment, scanning the waiting faces in the room. "Since my whole connection to Nico Rossi began with dating his daughter Angela, I'd like to be called Angelo in her honor of taking down her father."

Vera smiled, accentuating a face full of laugh lines. "I like that. And from what you told us about her, I think she would, too." Vera put out her hand again, taking Rafe's and her warm grasp. "It's nice to meet you, Angelo. Now go change so we can catch some bad guys."

Rafe followed her orders, disappearing into his

room upstairs to swap out his jeans and T-shirt for a clean black suit. He tied the tie and straightened the lapels. He was used to chef whites splattered in sauce. Running his fingers through his curls, he placed the black, small, brimmed hat on his head. His reflection still showed himself. Maybe he should put on a wig, too, he thought. But when he returned downstairs, Jeremy handed him a pair of large black sunglasses.

"Nobody will recognize you," Jeremy said. "Remember to have a servant attitude. You are a chauffeur to a very wealthy woman. There can be no ego, Rafe. Full humility."

Rafe folded his hands at his front and bowed his head. "How's that?"

Jeremy laughed. "I don't recognize you already. Are you sure I'm talking to Rafe Sinclair, ego extraordinaire?"

"Give me some credit. I'm trying here." Rafe pulled on his tight tie. He hated ties.

Jeremy sobered and helped him loosen it. "You're right, you are. So remember, when the time comes for Vera to take out her gun—" Jeremy tapped his cheek, "—be a peach…and duck."

VERA SHUT down the phone that Jeremy had given her and pocketed it in the white suit coat. She believed she had her plan in place and had figured out where Nico Rossi would spend Friday evening. One of his pseudo-legit organizations was having a fundraiser holiday tonight. He would be the guest of honor at the pharmaceutical gala that offered more than its claim for healing diabetes. It offered a cover to all their largest benefactors.

"When you reach the city, take Park Avenue," she instructed her driver. "There's an event at the Grand I plan to be at."

"Oh, you're talking to me now," Rafe replied snidely from behind the wheel. "You've been ignoring me for an hour."

Vera bit back a smile. "I wasn't ignoring you. I was getting into my character and doing a little research on the best way to do that without my team. Typically, I would have at least a few weeks to read up on all the files of the people I would be interacting with. Usually, my handler gets them to me." But Tangen seemed to be checked out. Vera hoped he was all right but knew if the man went dark, he had a good reason.

"Interesting. Was there a file on me?" Rafe asked.

"A very lengthy one. I had to go through *all* your girlfriends. Wow. Just wow."

"*All* of them?" Rafe turned his head to look at her.

"Eyes on the road, *Angelo*." Vera checked her face and neck in the compact mirror Mel had given her. The woman had more makeup than a cosmetologist for a Broadway musical. And yet, Mel appeared to use none of it, at least not for a long time. She stocked Vera up with enough to last a few weeks while under character. "We can't have any accidents. One mishap will shut us down."

"But seriously, do you really have a list of all my friends?"

"Not all of them. I was missing a file on Gus Vargas. Imagine my surprise when I showed up at Creare and found a stranger I didn't know about working there. And not just any stranger but the son of a crooked businessman. Not to mention he was walking down the snowy streets with one of Rossi's goons. Tell me why you're friends with him? Because you *are* judged by your acquaintances, and that one's a doozy."

"Gus is clean and trustworthy. I know his father isn't always on the up and up, but when Gus takes over, he plans to clean house. He's just waiting."

"Then explain his connection to Rossi."

Rafe drove quietly for a few minutes without answering. From behind, all Vera could do was wonder if he was attempting to come up with an excuse or if he really didn't know the answer.

"It's okay to admit you may not know someone as well as you think you do," she said.

"I've known Gus since the day his father gave me a job in one of his restaurants. We were instant friends, even though we were from different classes. His father would joke that I was Gus's little project, but Gus never made me feel that way. Instead, I think I was a way for Gus to separate himself from the expectations his father had for him."

"Sounds altruistic. So, if you don't mind, he's still a suspect for me."

"And if you don't mind, I'm going to disagree with you. I might even prove you wrong."

Having Rafe messing up her case was the last thing she needed. "Let me do the investigating, please. Stay in your character, or I will have to cut you loose. One wrong move means death. And I don't just mean for the case. The second Rossi suspects I am not who I say I am, he will put a bullet in my head."

"He would shoot an old lady?"

"He would shoot his own grandmother." Vera

thought of the file images from the last heist. Someone lost their beloved family member all because Rossi needed to keep finding ways to make his money.

"Speaking of grandmother," Rafe spoke through the rearview mirror. "I still can't believe I'm looking at you." He shook his head and said, "It's really you under all that makeup and fake skin. You'll have no problem convincing anyone, fancy Mercedes or not. Have I mentioned I feel like I'm driving a tank through these city streets? But I know what you're saying about cars completing the image. My Porsche plays a big part in the picture I portray to people."

"You mean all the women." Vera knew she sounded petty. Worse. She sounded like a jealous teenager.

Why was she jealous?

"Sure," Rafe said with a shrug. He took the next turn. "You're right. The ladies do love my car. But I didn't buy it for picking up chicks. I was on my way to becoming the hottest chef in town. Just like you, I needed the persona to make the world see me that way. When Creare first opened with Mel and Chris running the place, I was offered my own television series. I would have traveled the world, showcasing all of Vargas' cuisines at all his establishments. My car contributed to all that."

"But Papa Vargas wanted his money back."

Rafe looked in the mirror again. "How do know about the money?"

"File, remember?"

Rafe blew out a deep breath. "No wonder you pinned me as a suspect."

"*Numero uno.*"

"Do you still think that?"

"Did you take the offer for the show?"

"I'm driving *you* around, aren't I? Not to mention I'm still running Creare, at least for a few more months. So, no. I turned the offer down. I wanted, no, I *needed,* to make it on my own as a chef. And I did. No amount of money from Paul Vargas or Nico Rossi could have given me the name I made for myself."

"Nico offered you money, too?" This was news to her.

"You don't own a restaurant in the city without the mob checking you out. But I made sure everyone knew I was clean and couldn't be bought."

"Do you think he knows you ran off with his daughter?"

"Doubt it. I'd be dead already."

"The man is patient. He doesn't just go in for the kill. He destroys a person first. When did Creare start to go under?"

"I don't know. I suppose after the girls sold me the place."

"So, you didn't own it with Mel and Chris?"

"No, they wouldn't make me a partner. I strictly worked for them as their chef. When Mel sold her portion, she sold it to me. Chris signed her part over to me when she married Marcus. She's wealthy. She doesn't need the business. Not like I do."

"Exactly. Perhaps Rossi has been biding his time, waiting for the deathblow. He's been ruining your business and sitting back to watch you squirm this whole time. And now, he's using it as a front for his next heist. He'll blame the whole thing on you, and all roads *will* lead to you. He'll make sure of it."

Rafe shook his head. "He won't be able to. I run my business clean as a whistle. I have every invoice from the day I took over, and I only work with reputable companies. After I took Vargas's money, I vowed never again. I saw how my life was no longer my own. Being indebted to someone stole my future. When Creare was succeeding, I was finally able to pay off that debt. I am free and clear and mean to stay that way. Even if the restaurant goes under."

Vera still couldn't get over the missing link. "So, Gus Vargas came on to help you save Creare out of the kindness of his heart? And he just gave you money to buy Mel's portion?"

"Absolutely. He offered. Like I said, we've been friends since the day we met. He's the only person who I have been able to trust completely with *everything*. Even my son."

"I hope so. Because you gave him the keys to the castle. Are you sure he's not a Trojan horse who will strike when you are looking the other way? Like right now while Creare is closed down?"

"He's done an amazing job managing the place. Aside from him buying some cheaper meat to save a buck, I can't complain. Why are you saying this?"

"Because he is Suspect Number Two. Perhaps the two of you are in this together."

Rafe braked so fast, Vera felt her belt buckle lock up into a choke hold. He took the next right, speeding down the slick street. Flurries of snow hit the windshield at a fast rate.

"I said no accidents," Vera shouted. "What are you doing?"

"Proving you wrong." He took the next right, and she knew he was taking her to Creare.

"I have someplace to be. This gala has already

started. Time is short. I need to be there to gather intel. I don't have time for you to protect your friend. If he's not guilty, then he has nothing to worry about."

"Right. Because people haven't been arrested for crimes they didn't do. I'm going to end this right now."

"You can't give my identity away." Vera leaned forward as far as she could. She put her hands on the front seats. "Please listen to me. I can't risk blowing my cover."

"You won't. I'm sure no one is at Creare. I'm going to show you all the work Gus has done. It's all been legit."

Rafe took the next street and drove two blocks until Creare came into view. Only, the place was not only open.

It was packed.

"I don't understand," Rafe mumbled. "I told Monroe to close down. Who's cooking?"

Vera checked the time on her watch. Most attendees at the gala would be already introduced. She couldn't walk in after the largest benefactors were seated.

"Can we come back after the gala?" Vera asked.

"No way. I want to know who is running my

kitchen." Rafe sneered. He pulled the car over to a side street and up to his regular parking space.

Another car was parked in his spot.

Rafe hit the steering wheel and jammed the Mercedes into *park*. He jumped from the car, ripping the hat off his head. Running up the rear entrance, he pulled the door wide.

"This is not good," Vera said aloud, also exiting the car to catch up to him. She reached the door just as it closed on her.

Vera pulled the door wide just in time to hear Rafe yell louder than she'd ever heard him, "Get out of my kitchen!"

CHAPTER 8

*R*afe hadn't seen his kitchen full of employees in nearly a year.

Until now.

Everywhere he looked, he watched a full team bustling around, from pastry chefs to sous chefs, from line cooks to servers pushing through the double doors with their orders for them. But he knew not a one.

"I said I want everyone out of my kitchen right now! All of you! Out!" Rafe pointed to the double doors as the team stopped their work to stare at him. They looked at each other and shrugged.

"Who are you? And stop your yelling in my kitchen," the imposter head chef with his white toque said as he stepped forward from the ovens. He held a large knife with a white porcelain handle. Rafe recognized it as his own.

"Give that to me." Rafe held out his hand, ready to blow his top. If they thought he was yelling now, they hadn't seen anything yet.

"Answer the question."

"I am the owner of this restaurant. This is *my* kitchen, and that is *my* knife. Now give it to me."

The swinging doors opened, and Gus stepped in. "Rafe? I thought I heard you yelling." He let the doors swing behind him as he slowly approached. "I thought you were going to be away for a few weeks. Monroe told me you weren't around. Glad to see you back. But what happened?"

"I'd like an answer to that question as well. My directions to Monroe were shut down." Rafe looked around for the pantry chef. "Where is he?"

"Look. I know you're not going to like this, but I had to let him go." Gus frowned at Rafe with a shake of his head. "He lacked vision. And with you gone, we just couldn't agree on what to do."

"Meaning, he wanted you to shut down like my instructions said."

Gus grabbed Rafe's forearm. "Come see this."

Rafe pulled his arm away, but Gus kept walking to the doors and pushed one wide open to reveal the dining room—the completely full dining room. Every table was being used, and there were people waiting at the doors for seats. Rafe hadn't seen Creare look this busy since Chris left.

The air in his lungs rushed out at the site. Part of Rafe wanted to jump for joy at what this meant. Creare was going to make it. But the other part of him felt like his own knife was in his back. He had explicitly told Monroe to shut the place down. It was more than him not being here to run the restaurant. It was also the fact that Creare was being set up for criminal activity. Having it closed would show he had nothing nefarious planned, and Creare wouldn't be used by anyone else either.

But Gus ignored his orders.

Rafe's stomach twisted with a sick feeling that Vera might be right about his friend.

"Who are these people?" Rafe asked.

"They're customers. It's what you wanted. It's why you hired me!" Gus let the door close on them and stepped back into the kitchen.

"No. Who are all these workers? I didn't hire any of them. Where did they come from?"

The imposter head chef backed up, placing the knife on the counter. He pulled at his apron strings to remove the cloth. Bunching it up, he tossed it to the counter. "I can't work in these conditions."

Rafe burst out with a harsh laugh. "Good. Get out of here. I'm the head chef. Not you. Go find your own kitchen."

Before the chef could move to the rear exit, Gus stepped in front of him. "Wait. We seem to have a misunderstanding. Gerald, go back to work. I will fix this. Rafe has just been caught by surprise. He was out of town and didn't know I brought you in." To Rafe, he said, "Can we go into your office and talk?"

"This is my office. So start talking."

Gus glanced around at the gawking staff. "Get back to work, all of you." He peered at something behind Rafe and squinted, but then looked back at Rafe and said, "All right. After you hired that singer, I saw that maybe music would bring people in. When Roxie didn't show back up for work again, no big surprise there, I hired a few other singers. I came into work, prepared to tell you, except Monroe told me that you left a message to close the doors. We had already made such great progress with Roxie, I didn't want to lose all the people who were hearing about us. Word-of-mouth spreads fast, and it was our one shot."

Rafe folded his arms. "You're still not telling me where these workers came from."

"They're doing a great job."

The fact that Gus refused to answer the question gave Rafe all the information he needed. "Let me guess. You called in a favor to your daddy. Or I should say, *I* am now indebted to him *again*."

"I really wish you would stop looking at it that way. He has treated you like a son since the day he gave you a job. He took you under his wing and gave you a future."

"He owned me."

"I know it felt that way, but he's just a business-man. Every decision he makes has to have something in it for him. He thought you would work for him. When you chose to work for Mel and Chris instead, he had to call the loan due. It's business."

"He never said it was a loan. But fine. I paid it off. Every last penny for the tuition and for the car. And now here I am, once again owing him. Tell me, Gus. Just how much is all of this going to cost me this time?" Rafe waved his hand at all the employees standing around with unsure expressions on their faces.

"It doesn't have to cost you anything. Creare would make an excellent addition to the Vargas line.

I knew that when I gave you the money for you to buy Mel's portion. Creare can become what it was always meant to be. A five-star restaurant in the heart of New York City. Clientele from all over the world would come. You most likely would have your offer of a TV series back in your lap. You'll be famous, Rafe. Can't you see it? Your name will be in lights. You might even get a book deal. Boy from the other side of the tracks now feeding those who rejected him."

Rafe stood stunned at each word coming out of his friend's mouth. "Was it true? What your father said? Was I always just your little project?"

"You were my friend. You *are* my friend. My *best* friend. Everything I have done for you is because I care about you. Do you think I have enjoyed watching you grow more and more depressed every day as your business has failed? I'm helping you the best way I know how. Using resources at my fingertips. They're there for the taking. Someday my father's line of businesses will be mine. Then you and I will be…"

"Will be what?" Rafe felt his throat close, and he thought for a moment he might cry. In all the years he had been friends with Gus, since the moment he stepped into the restaurant that Rafe was bussing tables at, Gus never made him feel different. Never made him feel less than him.

Until this moment.

"Partners. I was going to say partners."

"No, you weren't. You were going to say equal."

Gus blanched and dropped his gaze to the floor. He shook his head back and forth. "You're wrong," he said, but his voice lacked conviction.

"Mr. Sinclair," Vera spoke from behind. "We really need to be going. I am expected at this gala. Are you still accompanying me, or not? I'm beyond fashionably late."

"Who's the old lady?" Gus asked. He eyed Rafe from head to toe and back up again. "And why are you dressed in a suit? What's going on? And what is she talking about accompanying her to some gala?"

"It's nothing. And she's not some old lady. She's—"

Vera pushed past him with her arm extended. She presented her hand as though she meant for Gus to kiss it. "I am Winifred Winterbottom. I have expressed interest in purchasing Creare, and Mr. Sinclair has been kind enough to spend these last few days with me going over the particulars of the business."

The tables turned, and now Gus looked as

though he had been sucker punched. "What is she talking about, Rafe? You never said anything about finding a buyer. I would've done that for you. I would've bought it!"

Rafe nearly said Creare wasn't for sale, but the hard look Vera sent him reminded him they were in character. She was undercover, and one wrong word could blow that for her. As much as Rafe hated to admit it, she was right about Gus. Rafe had been too close to see his friend had ulterior motives.

"Please tell me you were not waiting in the wings to buy my restaurant? The cheaper choices of meat, the firing of servers, all of it...please tell me it wasn't so that I would sell to you. Were you setting me up?"

"I'm insulted that you would even suggest it. There was nothing wrong with the meat. Perhaps you're not as good of a chef as you claim."

If Vera didn't tug on his forearm, Rafe thought he might've slugged him. "Clock is ticking, Mr. Sinclair. I have people waiting for my presence. We must be on our way. Good day to you all."

Gus shouted across the kitchen. "I'm calling my father. Any transaction will be stopped immediately. He is first in line for any purchasing."

"Says who?" Rafe demanded.

Gus shook his head and tsked. "A good businessman always reads the fine print. I guess you're not only a horrible chef. You're an even worse businessman. My father knew it was only a matter of time until you lost this place."

"I haven't lost anything yet. And I'm not going to. Find another unsuspecting kid to be your project."

"Who? Grady? Now that you mention it, that might not be a bad idea."

Rafe took two steps before Vera pulled him back. "You leave him alone!"

Vera squeezed his arm. He could feel the warning in her grip. He couldn't lose it now. Too much was at stake. But Gus was threatening to use Grady. What would he do to the boy?

Rafe's chest constricted at all that could go wrong with one phone call.

"Please, Gus." Rafe heard the fear in his own voice. The smug smile on Gus's face told him he had won. The one thing Rafe had entrusted with no one else but Gus would be the one thing Gus would use against him. He would use Rafe's own son to control him. "Would you really hurt him?"

"Do you really want to find out?"

"Rafe," Vera said sternly. "It's time."

Rafe knew what she was saying. It wasn't time for a gala. It was time to find out who was really setting him up. He nodded at Vera but couldn't look at Gus. He turned to leave, but as he did, he caught sight of the chef tying his apron back on.

Gerald was now the new king of this domain, and everyone knew it.

Rafe locked his gaze on the man and walked up to the counter. The chef looked at Gus with raised eyebrows. A little fear in his eyes showed he thought Rafe was about to hit him. Slowly, Rafe reached out as though he meant to go for the man's throat. Then, with his other hand, he grabbed the hilt of his chef's knife and let it mold into his hand as it always had.

"This is mine. Get your own," Rafe said with a sneer. On pivot, he joined Vera at the exit.

As Rafe pulled out of the back parking lot, driving the Mercedes with Vera in the rear, he caught sight of Gus watching him go. But instead of the smug expression the man had before, Gus appeared worried. He rubbed the side of his forehead, and Rafe thought maybe Gus was having second thoughts about what he'd said. Rafe waited for him to brush away the graying hair at his temple as he always did when he was concerned. Then the smug smile returned, and Gus turned his back. He entered Creare, and Rafe had his answer.

VERA SAT in the backseat but wished she could be upfront in the passenger seat. Showing up at the hotel in the backseat was critical for her undercover character, but ignoring Rafe's obvious pain over losing his best friend reflected on her personal character. Checking her watch again, she wondered if she should seek a Plan B and forget about the gala tonight.

"I could research another event that Rossi will be at. I don't know if there will be one this close to the heist, but I can look."

No response came. Rafe continued to drive as though he hadn't heard a word she'd said. She nearly reached to see if there was a glass between them.

"Rafe?" she said, a bit louder.

"The name is Angelo. If anyone blows this tonight, it's going to be you."

Vera started to balk at his accusation but quickly smiled. His black curls peeked out beneath the cap he donned again. They brushed the collar of his suit coat that she knew he found constricting. The entire setup made him uncomfortable, but he wasn't complaining. Even while his personal life imploded, he stuck to the mission. She couldn't ask for a better undercover partner.

"I don't think I told you yet, but you look smart all dressed up." She leaned forward to rest her hand on his seat, capturing his rigid profile. "People might not buy that you're a chauffeur and think you're a guest."

Rafe reached to the seat beside him and picked up the sunglasses. He showed them to her and put them on his face, alleviating her concern. "I'll disappear into the shadows."

The snow flurries turned to a full storm, and the windshield wipers cut into the silence between them. She needed to ask if he was okay with how everything went down with Gus but also needed to remain focused on the plan.

"I was glad to see my disguise fooled Gus," she said.

"Me too, but I'm not surprised."

"Because it's that convincing?"

"No. Because Gus is a selfish fool. He's only focused on what's important to him. How did I miss that about him? What made me think he would treat me differently? And why would I ever think *he* would be different than everyone else?"

"How is he the same?" Vera felt unsure if Rafe's unloading was something she should be privy to. But she did have a case to solve and intel to collect. Without knowing it, Rafe could have the knowledge she needed to infiltrate this next heist. "Are all your friends cutthroat businessmen?"

Did any of them have ties to Creare? She held her tongue as she waited for Rafe to answer about how Gus was the same as everyone else.

Vera caught Rafe watching her in the rearview mirror. Even through the sunglasses, she sensed he was making a decision to trust her with something.

"How, Rafe?" She held his gaze.

He quickly broke the connection to watch the road. The hotel appeared ahead. He put the blinker on and parked at the curb. Righting his cap, he exited to escort her out, holding the door for her. At the entrance, he said under his breath. "They leave. Everyone leaves."

Vera paused as the doorman opened the door for her. Rafe's admission felt raw and personal. For some reason, he considered her to be safe to trust with his deepest fear.

As honored as that made her feel, she needed him

focused. He would be her eyes in the back of her head. Vera took his hand, demanding that he see her behind the makeup. She felt the need to assure him not everyone was untrustworthy. But she was the last person to make such a statement. She always worked alone. It was safer that way. But why?

Vera knew the answer to that and saw no other way. Keeping herself free of relationships gave the bad guys nothing to control her with. Rossi took her parents. But who else could he take after that?

No one.

Telling Rafe that not everyone leaves would be a lie. Some people *had* to leave. They had no other choice. He knew what it meant to be owned, but she knew how not to be.

"You're right, they do. And it hurts." Vera said, holding tight to his hand. "But those who matter most will show up when you need them again. Do you understand, Angelo?"

Rafe squeezed her hand, then brought it to his lips. "Ms. Winterbottom, you can count on me."

Vera felt the warmth of his touch linger even after he returned to park the car. It was time for them to part ways for the evening. They each had their roles to play and their goals to accomplish. But as she walked through the lobby and entered the ballroom, she rubbed her hand where his lips had been.

She was entering dangerous territory, both with the crowd of crooks before her and with seeing Rafe as anything but a means to an end.

"It can't be anything," she whispered to herself.

"What can't be?" a man asked beside her.

Vera realized she had spoken too loud and inwardly chastised her slipup. Another reason for going solo. She then wondered why she was even putting a pros and cons list together. First jealousy reared its head back at Mel's house, and now Vera's mind battled about finding a place for Rafe in her life?

"It can't be this glorious of an event. It's beautiful," she covered her faux pas. "And just look at all of those presents under the tree. Gold and silver wrapping. How exciting! I'm Winnifred Winterbottom. My late husband was a huge benefactor. Thank you for doing this event." She extended her hand to the man in his black-tie attire. Before he took it, Vera glanced off to her right and feigned seeing someone she knew. "Carl, I don't believe it's you! How long has it been?" She raced off in the direction she was facing, slipping into the crowd smoothly, leaving behind the man at the door.

Peering through a throng, she saw the man looking over heads for her, but a woman stepped up to him to ask a question, and he turned her way. Vera was safe to move about the room—for now. Get the intel and get out. Her swift cheetah instincts were kicking in.

Vera joined a group of ladies mingling by the enormous Christmas tree. She nodded her head to something one of them was saying and laughed at all the right places. To anyone watching, she looked to be part of the gang. But all the while, she gathered information from every group in every dark corner and at every table. Zeroing in on faces, Vera pulled up her mental files on each person. Years of memorization zipped across her mind's eye.

Johnny Warner: Bank robber for hire, grew up in Queens, divorced three times, loves his dog, a bloodhound, and owns a vacation home in the Caribbean that he claimed he received in his second divorce.

Sid Malcolm: Bar owner in the Bronx, launders money through it, married for twenty years to Jeanette and has three kids. In so deep, he'll never get out. If he tries, he'll go to jail for the rest of his life—if he doesn't conveniently die before the trial.

Vic Simons: Nico Rossi's brother-in-law, married into the business, assigned the dirty jobs, creepy tattoos from his neck down. He knows he'll be the fall guy if Rossi ever goes down.

The room was filled with people from her files. Everyone except for Nico Rossi.

It made no sense. According to her research, he was listed as a guest of honor. An alibi, perhaps? Send all his cronies in his stead while he's somewhere else sealing the deal? Vera could've ripped her wig off right then. She'd fallen for one of the oldest tricks in the book. She felt like an amateur.

Then she saw a familiar face and thought maybe she wasn't the only one.

Across the ballroom, Tangen whispered into a lady's ear, making her throw her head back and laugh. She touched his lapel fondly. Vera's handler also believed tonight's event held intel, and he was working the room.

Vera politely excused herself from the ladies and mingled with clusters along the way. She didn't want to make a beeline right to him, as that would alert the guards posted throughout. She could pick them out easily with how they all stood with both hands clasped over their potbellies and their shoulders punched out. Vera waited for Tangen to recognize her. He would be the only person here who would.

Knowing his observation skills, she figured he already had.

A server approached with their tray. "Chicken?" He halted in front of her.

Vera lost sight of Tangen. She pushed up on her tiptoes to look over the man's shoulder. "Oh, thank you."

He held out a piece of chicken skewered on a stick. "Napkin?"

Vera took the napkin, trying to move past the server quickly. One step back, and her handler had disappeared. Her gaze darted left to right, up and down the aisles. She dropped the food on one of the tables.

"Chicken?" The server asked another guest. "Napkin?"

As Vera's inward antenna sought her handler's face, the voice of the server warred for her attention. She turned around, targeting his back...and his head of black curls.

Rafe?

Vera controlled her every movement as she practically stomped back to him. He was not supposed to be in here. He was her getaway car. If something went wrong, she would be stranded. He was to remain with the staff and gather information from them.

From behind, she tapped him on the shoulder. "I'll take some chicken," she said, not bothering to hide the irritation in her voice.

Rafe turned around to hold out the tray.

Only it wasn't Rafe as she had thought.

Grady. The air rushed from her lungs as she was face-to-face with Rafe's son.

"What are you doing here?" she whispered.

"Excuse me? I'm working. Chicken?" A hint of nervousness threaded his words, and she realized he didn't recognize her. He wouldn't know Winnie. He'd left Mel's house before the decision was made to bring her out.

But why was he at this function? Is this what he meant, that he would take care of things on his own now? Was the boy trying to get close to his grandfather for a reason?

Vera studied the waistband of his tuxedo with a quick glance up and down. Was the boy packing a gun? This could be terrible once Rossi arrived. Without knowing what Grady planned, Vera considered revealing herself to him. But that could be deadly for them both if a guard caught on. She wouldn't be able to control Grady's reaction.

"Yes, I'll take a chicken." He handed her one on

the skewer, and she shoved it in her mouth. Before he could turn, she said, "I'll take another."

"Um, sure." He handed her a second piece.

Vera bit the meat off the stick fast. She then held out her hand for another.

"Another?"

"Just keep them coming." She spoke with her mouth full.

"I don't think I'm supposed to—"

"Look, sonny. I paid a lot of money to be here. Just keep them coming." Vera spoke in her most crotchety voice she could muster. Three more pieces, and his tray was nearly empty. He'd have to return to the kitchen for more soon. Hopefully, before Rossi arrived. "Do you have any of those crab puffs?" she asked.

Grady frowned and looked around the room, obviously not excited about leaving the ballroom. "I can go check."

"I'll wait right here."

The boy turned and made his way back to the crowd. As soon as he headed into the kitchen, Vera brought her wristwatch to her face.

Pushing a button on the side, she spoke quickly. "Get to the kitchen and intercept your son. He's up to something."

She could only hope Rafe was listening. Eyeing the doors to the kitchen, she watched servers come and go with their trays. The surrounding murmurs grew louder, and soon everyone in the ballroom applauded. A glance at the entrance doors explained why.

The guest of honor had arrived.

CHAPTER 9

*H*ad he heard Vera right? Grady was here? In the building? And heading to the kitchen?

Rafe had no time to process the details. His only concern was finding his son. He hated leaving the rest of the chauffeur crew but saw no other way. In the little time he had spent with them, they talked his ear off, sharing about some interesting places they had brought their employers to.

"Where you going?" one of them asked Rafe as he separated himself from them.

"I'm hungry. I'm hoping I can convince one of the waitresses to slip me some caviar or something."

The group of men laughed. "Bring some back to share."

Rafe pointed to the guy. "You got it."

When he hit the inside hall, he took off running. Working in kitchens his whole adult life, he guessed correctly on the location of the kitchen, based on the placement of the ballrooms. Entering the steam filled room, he watched servers come and go from the swinging doors with their trays. He grabbed one and got in line. All the while, he searched their faces, looking for a familiar one.

"Didn't I just give you the crab puffs?" a chef in his sweaty polyester whites demanded. "Oh, never mind. I thought you were someone else." The chef placed skewered dumplings on Rafe's tray.

"Can you go faster?" Rafe didn't hide his anxiety.

"Awfully demanding, aren't you?" He dropped the last two on the tray. "Next!"

Rafe was out the door with his tray immediately, nearly colliding with another server entering. Standing on the other side of the door, the guests had lined up on two sides of the ballroom, leaving a walkway open for the honored guests as they made their way to their tables.

Rafe paid no mind to the goings on. He searched for every server in their black suits until finally he found the one he was looking for.

Grady stood in front of Vera as she stuffed her

wrinkled face with crab puffs. He held his tray out but looked beyond her. Rafe followed his gaze to Nico Rossi. Then Grady handed the tray to Vera and moved toward the mobster. Rafe jumped to reach Rossi first. Whatever his son had planned couldn't happen.

Grady reached inside his coat, and Rafe picked up his steps. If the boy whipped out a gun in this place, everyone else would, too. One glance back at Vera showed she was ready to blow her cover to stop him as well. Rafe shook his head, wanting her to know he had it covered.

But did he?

Feeling inside his own coat, his hand met the hilt of his knife. He couldn't very well remove that either.

"Excuse me," a woman spoke, stopping him short. "I'll take one of those." She reached for a skewered dumpling. Biting into it, she scrunched her nose. "Never mind." She placed it back on his tray and reached for something else.

"Here, take it." Rafe shoved it at her, leaving her behind and gasping at his nerve. But Grady was now closer to Rossi. Elbowing through the crowd, he reached the makeshift corridor just as Grady stepped in front of Rossi and stopped him cold. The crowd inhaled at once, including Rafe. His heart clenched and lodged in his throat.

"Well, hello, Grady," Nico Rossi said slowly. "What a surprise to see you here." He held up his hand to ward off his men, all reaching inside their own coats for their guns. "Join me at my table. We have a lot to talk about."

Grady removed his hand from his coat and followed Nico to the table. He took the seat beside him but sat rigid and upright. He said something under his breath, but Rafe couldn't make it out.

This was the moment Rafe had done everything he could to avoid. But Grady was correct in that Rossi knew who he was. Had he always known? Was Vera right about Rossi biding his time to take down Rafe?

He turned to look her way, but she now was gone. She had asked him to cut Grady off, but he had failed. Circling the ballroom, he searched for her and thought how his words of her being able to count on him now fell flat. The idea of letting her down made him feel just as sick as his son sitting down with Nico Rossi did. But if his son could do it, then so could he.

With each step closer to the table, Rafe hoped he would get to the bottom of this case for Vera, even if it meant Rossi stuck his goons on him. If someone was setting him up, he had a right to know before they put a bullet in his head.

He reached ten feet from Rossi's chair before three of those goons stepped forward, reaching for the guns.

"Let me through," Rafe said. "Call off your men, Rossi."

Nico turned, eyebrows raised. He scratched his chin, then waved a finger. The men stepped back, but not away.

"I said I could handle this myself," Grady said, anger threading his voice. "What are you doing here? Why did you follow me?"

Rafe thought it best to let Grady think he was here for him. "To stop you from making the biggest mistake of her life. But I can see I'm too late."

Nico chuckled. "I disagree, Mr. Sinclair. Your boy is right where he belongs. Beside me. It's where he always should have been, but you stole his legacy from him."

"I kept him safe. From you. Angela knew you would destroy him. I won't let you do that to him. Not now and not ever. Grady, come with me. Please."

"Sit down, Mr. Sinclair. Grady is not going

anywhere, and neither are you. We have a lot to discuss." To the crowd, standing by and gawking, Nico waved his hand. "Carry on with the festivities. Enjoy the evening. It is a good night. My grandson, Grady Rossi, has come home." Nico began clapping, inviting the rest of the crowd to join him. Soon, smiles and cheers went out and people returned to their mingling, oblivious to what the statement meant for Grady.

A life of crime and servitude.

Rafe figured he would not be leaving this hotel alive, and it was only a matter of time before his assassination was ordered. He had nothing to lose and wouldn't hold anything back.

"Did you kill her? Did you kill your daughter? Grady's mother?" When Rossi didn't respond, Rafe pushed on. "Did you sabotage my restaurant? Did you cause Creare to fail just to hurt me? To get me back for taking your daughter from you?"

Nico turned to Grady. "Do you see the power I have? I am making your own father squirm, and I haven't lifted a finger. He stole this power from you. Imagine who you would be today if you had all the money and status you were born into. Andrews," Nico said with a snarl. "It's Rossi, and it always has been." Nico looked back at Rafe. "You gave up your rights. You are nothing to the boy. Thanks to Angela for making sure of that. She may have told you it was to protect the boy from me, but it was you all along."

"No. I won't let you tarnish her name."

"To answer your question, she wasn't supposed to be in the car that night. In fact, she wasn't supposed to be with you at all. Since the day she was born, she was promised to someone else. When you came along, you ruined our plans. The Rossi and Vargas families would have been united."

"Vargas?" Rafe attempted to hide his surprise. The workings of his mind processed through what the man wasn't saying. "Gus?"

"You stole his bride from him. I'm surprised he kept you so close and didn't kill you. But I appreciate the man's patience. He'll have his day. Soon."

If Rafe hadn't seen how Gus betrayed him already, he would have denied every word that Nico spewed. Had their friendship been a complete ruse? Rafe thought back to the day he met Angela and how their relationship came to be. She had come to the restaurant he worked at, saying she was meeting her boyfriend there. Only her boyfriend never showed up. Rafe convinced her to go out with him instead.

"Gus never...he didn't tell me." Rafe remembered

Gus's car broke down that night and that was why he didn't show up at the restaurant. He had texted him, saying he wanted him to meet someone but never said another word about it after that night. Not that Rafe gave him the chance. Two weeks later, Rafe was in love. Two months later, he took Angela from the city, running away with her. Just how mad was Gus? Enough to kill him?

"I see you're putting it together." Nico smiled. "Now if you'll excuse us, I have some catching up to do with my grandson. It's time."

Rafe looked at his son. "Grady, please come with me."

Grady shook his head. "Like the man said. It's time. You shouldn't have come here. I'm sorry, Rafe."

Rafe? The way he said his name felt so final, like calling him Dad was over. It was the only thing that made the whole situation bearable.

"You'll be owned. You'll never have your life back. That's all I've ever wanted for you. For you to be free."

"I know you think that, but have I really been? I now have a way to have the life I'm supposed to."

"This is about money? Look around you. There's so much money in this room, it stinks. But the scent you smell is blood. Be careful what you agree to, son." With nothing else to say, Rafe pushed back his chair.

"Not so fast," Nico said, waving to one of his men with the crook of his finger. "My brother-in-law wants to have a word with you...out back. Vic will take good care of you. Thank you for stopping by, Mr. Sinclair. And thank you for the use of your restaurant. It's going to be a smashing event. Too bad you won't be around to see the fireworks."

Rafe realized Creare's connection to the next heist. It would be the place that blew up the block. Rafe reached for his watch, needing to push the button that would alert Vera to the plan. But before he could, Vic grabbed his wrist and swung his arm up behind him.

"You've worn out your welcome. Time to go." Vic didn't push through the crowd but took him out through the kitchen, using Rafe's face to push the door open.

"Get out of my kitchen!" The chef yelled. But when he saw who dragged Rafe, he ordered his cooks to get back to work and forget what they saw.

Rafe would get no help from the kitchen staff.

Vic pushed him outside into an alley, throwing him up against the brick wall of the building. He pushed his arm into Rafe's neck, cutting off his air supply. So, it would be death by asphyxiation? Less noisy than a gunshot, he supposed. Stars burst from Rafe's eyes, and he thought he heard his neck crunch. He definitely heard himself choking. No matter how much he pushed at Vic, the man was unmovable.

In the next second, release came, and air rushed back into Rafe's lungs. It took a moment for his vision to clear. Then he saw something white flash around Vic. Rafe realized Vic was being beaten up by an old woman.

Winifred Winterbottom to be exact.

She kicked him and brought him to his knees. But what Vera didn't see was the gun at his ankle that he instantly went for.

"Gun!" Rafe shouted, reaching into his coat for the hilt of his knife.

Vic withdrew the weapon and pointed it into Vera's stomach just as Rafe let his knife fly. The white porcelain handle protruded from Vic's arm as the man fell to the ground, and his gun went off.

Vera threw her body down on his arm and wrestled the gun away. Before she jumped to her feet, she pulled the knife back out, causing Vic to scream in pain.

"Run," she ordered through gritted teeth.

Around the corner, the Mercedes awaited. This time, Vera jumped in behind the wheel. With the keys in the ignition, she had it started and pulled out onto the street before Rafe realized what he had done. He sat in the passenger seat and looked over at the blood on her pantsuit—Arlene's pantsuit. So much for Vera keeping blood off it.

Except Vera hadn't stabbed Vic.

He had.

VERA GRIPPED the steering wheel and drove past the hotel entrance slowly, looking for any sign of mayhem after what had just happened. All she could see were men loading up the presents she'd seen at the gala. Gifts for Rossi, no doubt. As if the lowlife needed any of them. It wouldn't be long before this place was crawling with cops. Someone would be sure to phone it in, and all these criminals would be heading for the hills.

"Do me a favor?" she said, picking up her speed, though she didn't know where she could go.

"What?" Rafe whispered beside her. He had his eyes glued to her clothes.

"Never try to save me again."

"He was going to kill you, Vera. I couldn't…" Rafe gulped and tried to speak again. "I…"

"You should have run."

"Run? You're kidding. I wasn't going to leave you behind. I promised you I wouldn't. I promised that you could count on me. I meant it. Did you even know he had the gun?"

Vera hated to admit it, but she didn't. She knew Vic had one on him, but she didn't know he had already retrieved it. "Just don't do that again."

"Why not? It's what you would've done for me."

"It's my job. I'm trained thoroughly for every kind of assault and attack."

"One more second, and you would have been dead. Then what? At least now I have a fighting chance to survive. Vic dragged me out there to kill me. And now Rossi's got Grady. The boy sold his soul. For what?" Rafe dropped his head in his hands. The pain in his voice cut Vera deeper than Rafe's knife had cut Vic's arm.

"Don't take it personally. Grady's going through something. He thinks this is the way to fix it. But it's his lesson to learn, and it has nothing to do with you. Someday he may seek you out again. Be ready for that day."

"If he's alive to. Besides, I'm a dead man at this

point and won't be here to help him. Rossi will not call back his goons against me. And he's not going to like what I did to Vic. Vic's going to tell Rossi that an old woman took him down. Your cover's blown as well."

"I'll get another. I have many to choose from. It's my job. It's what I do." Although without her team, her choices were limited. She'd like to know what happened to Tangen in there. She never saw him again. Why would her handler skip out on her? He had to have seen her. Now he was not only ignoring her phone calls, but he was also avoiding her when he *saw* her? Had the FBI told him to separate himself from her because she went rogue? That was the only excuse possible. Still, with or without her team, she would do her job.

"Well, you may not want me to save you, but I'm grateful you saved me back there. My lights were about to go out."

"I almost missed it. I was listening to another conversation while you were talking to Rossi. Two of his men were saying this next heist is the biggest one yet. The men are a little nervous they won't be able to pull it off. They said something about their man going missing, and they need him. They also said they need the money from this heist to finance something bigger, whatever that is. I'm still missing certain details to put this all together and make it make sense."

"When I was sitting with Rossi, he told me they're using my restaurant for the explosion. They're going to blow it up. At the time, he thought I wouldn't be around to see it happen. It can't happen at all, Vera."

"Creare is the location for the detonation. Fifty pounds of C-4 could take out a mile in every direction. I can work with this." Vera pulled over to a side street and parked.

"What are you doing?" Rafe watched her turn her cell phone on.

"I need a map." She widened the screen's image.

Rafe pointed to where his restaurant was located. From there, Vera drew a circle equidistant to the restaurant about a mile out in all directions. Whatever Rossi was after could be found in the area around Creare.

"The day I saw Gus walking with one of Rossi's men, where were they coming from?"

Rafe shrugged. "He said he had to pay a bill. I figure he was out mailing the check. I didn't ask. Though, I wish I had. I gave the man way too much trust. And way too much leeway with the business. All this time, he was tanking Creare."

"What do you mean? It looked like he wanted the restaurant to make it. Not destroy it."

"You were right about his allegiance to his family. Rossi told me Gus was supposed to marry Angela and unite their families into one big business."

Vera whistled slowly. "And you got in the way and ruined it. Paul Vargas enticed you to come back by paying for your school and buying you a fancy car. He must've seen your potential as a chef and thought you owed him. He missed out on an alliance with the Rossi clan, so would make his own dynasty on your back."

"While his son kept me close, earning my trust. Knowing someday he would have his retribution. All this time, he knew where Grady was, which means Rossi knew as well." Rafe pulled at his tie, trying to loosen it to no avail.

Vera reached over and tugged on the knot, giving the man a reprieve from the torture he was experiencing. He covered her hand and held her still.

"Why would you rather die than have me save you?" he asked her.

She felt as though his tie choked her now instead. Police sirens raced by, heading in the direction of the hotel, but neither of them moved. "You don't understand." She wasn't sure if she could explain it herself.

"He killed your parents. If Rossi thinks you care about anyone, or if anyone cares about you, he'll kill them, too. Am I right?"

"Yes. And just for the fun of it."

"And you think by me trying to save you means I care about you."

"I wouldn't presume such a thing."

"Then that means Rossi will know *you* care about *me*."

Vera dropped her gaze, unable to look at him. He voiced what she couldn't even think about. At some point along with their travels, she'd let Rafe in. "It means nothing. But yes, something in me wants to get to know you. At first, it was silly jealousy of Mel."

"Mel? Why? She's married. And has a baby."

Vera shrugged. "I saw a picture in your office and the way you looked at her...it was more than friendship."

Rafe flashed a grin. A blush spread out from his neck onto his cheeks. "I liked her. A lot. But it was never anything other than friendship. She saw right through me. Just like you did. She called me out on it, just like you did. I'm surprised you would have anything other than disgust for me."

"I tried to. But when I saw Vic killing you, it felt like Rossi was taking another person from me." Air rushed from Vera's lungs at her admission. "Nothing can happen between us. No one can ever know how I feel."

Vera needed Rafe to understand this right then and there.

"And what if I feel the same way?"

"You're just saying that. You don't mean it. It's your adrenaline after what just happened. You think you have to reciprocate these feelings. You don't."

"You're wrong. In fact, Mel noticed it right away. I denied it, of course, but deep down, I knew she was right. I liked you. I *like* you."

"Well, stop right now." Vera pulled her hand from his grasp. "You can do it. You know you can. You love 'em and leave 'em all the time. You said yourself that you're incapable of having a long-term relationship."

"I never said I was incapable. I said I wouldn't let myself. There's a difference. Angela and I were going to get married and be a family. I am fully capable."

"I'll have to take your word for it because we're not going to find out. I'm going to do my job and keep you safe. And I'm going to infiltrate Rossi's plan to blowup a huge chunk of New York City. And then

I will put the handcuffs on the man once and for all. I have wanted it for so long."

"Even more than love?"

"Yes." She faced forward. "I can't be derailed."

"We want the same things, Vera. That makes us stronger."

"It doesn't change the fact that I will still be another person that leaves you." At his silence, she pulled back out into traffic, satisfied her answer would put this conversation to rest.

"Take a right," he said.

Vera listened, but asked, "Where are we going? We can't go to your apartment. Rossi will have all his men canvassing the place."

"To Chris's apartment. She still keeps it for when she visits. Her friend Sam lives there. We'll be able to get cleaned up and decide who you're going to be next, because you can't be an old lady anymore."

Vera agreed that Winifred Winterbottom needed to go away for a while. "And you need to hide out. You can't be anywhere near Creare. They'll be waiting for you. Once I'm in another disguise, I can stop in and check things out. If it will be the location of the blast, that will be a lot of C-4 to unload. They won't be able to hide that in the corners."

"Who will you be?" Rafe asked. "Would you bring Roxie back out?"

"Too risky. Word would reach Nico, and he might be suspicious enough to call off the heist. I have another idea. It will require a little research, but the more I think about it, this is the way I'm going to go."

"Care to explain? Pull onto this side street and park. Her apartment's across the street."

Vera squeezed the Mercedes between two vehicles to hide the plates. Looking into the rearview mirror, she slipped her fingers beneath the wig and lifted it off her head. Tossing the white hair in the backseat, she pulled the pins from her bun and let her blond hair go free. Before she stepped from the car, she was nearly devoid of all evidence of Winnie.

"Are you going to tell me who you'll become next?" Rafe asked on the sidewalk. "Or are you keeping it a big secret?"

Vera faced him with a big smile that never felt more confident. "You're looking at her. When I slap those cuffs on Nico Rossi, it will be as Special Agent Vera Sharp."

CHAPTER 10

*R*oxie Moon was stunning and energetic. Winifred Winterbottom was lovely and sophisticated. But Vera Sharp was all those things and so much more. Rafe felt honored to walk beside this strong woman capable of catching criminals with her quick hands and soothing a room with her powerful voice. He felt inadequate beside her as they crossed the street and approached Chris's apartment building. He moved to hold the door for her, but the doorman stepped out and took the opportunity from him.

"Rafe. Long time no see," Charlie said, tipping his brimmed hat. He tugged his coat closed against the midnight chill. "Christina arrived a few hours ago. She didn't tell me you were coming."

"She doesn't know. In fact, I didn't realize she was in town. Maybe this isn't a good place to stay." Rafe glanced Vera's way. His mind whirled with other possibilities of where they could go this late at night.

"Nonsense. She would be offended if I turned you away. Go on up. I'll ring her to let her know you're on your way."

"Thanks, Charlie. But if anyone else asks, we were never here."

"I understand. I saw nothing." Charlie winked at Vera and pushed the button for the elevator. The doors opened, but Rafe held his breath until they closed, and they were officially out of sight.

At Chris's apartment, Rafe knocked once, but the door swung wide before he could knock again.

Chris stood in front of him, and her long blond hair swayed as she reached for him with both arms. "Mel told me everything going on. Marcus and I just arrived. We've been trying to reach you, but you haven't been answering your phone. We went over to Creare, and you were nowhere to be seen. Who's running the place now?"

"It's a long story. I'll explain it all. I haven't kept my phone on me, so I couldn't be tracked. Mel said she was going to call you, but I didn't know you would fly up here from Georgia."

"Of course we would." Chris stepped back and waved to her husband to join them. "Marcus has a lot of information to give to you about this Nico Rossi. We hope the details from his organized crime coalition can fill in some blanks for you."

Vera said, "I would appreciate any information you can give me. Perhaps you have some things that I don't have in my file." Vera extended her hand. "Special Agent Vera Sharp, FBI."

Chris's eyes widened at the blood on Vera's clothes. "Are you okay?"

"I'm fine. It's not mine."

"Oh, thank God. You're not as tall as me, but my friend Sam has some clothes you can change into."

"I would appreciate that, too. Thank you."

"Follow me. Rafe, make yourself comfortable with Marcus out here while I help Vera…um, I mean Agent Sharp."

"Vera is fine," Vera said, following Chris past the kitchen and down the hall.

Chris continued, "My old roommate Sam, who still lives here, is out of town with some friends, so her room is free."

Rafe settled onto the couch across from Marcus, who took one of the white chairs by the fireplace. The decor of the apartment hadn't changed since the last time Rafe had visited. A baby grand piano stood by the double windows, and the white furniture blended in with the white walls. Chris and Mel used to live here together long before they started the restaurant. When Mel ran away to the city, Chris took her in. Chris herself had come to the city to be a ballerina, but more importantly, to escape her own organized crime family. As the sole heiress to the fortune, she now was cleaning up the mess her family had made in the South.

"I have a son," Rafe blurted to Marcus.

Marcus leaned forward to rest his elbows on his knees. The man usually wore a suit and his dark hair slicked back, which gave him a mobster look as well. But he was anything but. He and Rafe grew up on similar sides of the tracks. But where Rafe fell into bribes, Marcus fought against them. He used his every penny to become an attorney and created his coalition to clean up the streets. Rafe had only ever wanted to be a chef, but being in the presence of Vera and Marcus, he wondered what good his profession was doing for the world.

"Go on. Tell me about your son," Marcus said.

"I gave him up for adoption when he was a baby.

His mother was killed in a car accident. She was the daughter of Nico Rossi. When I spoke with Nico tonight, he led me to believe that it was not an accident, and that I was the one who was supposed to die. I thought I was hiding Grady, my son, from the man and his lifestyle. It turns out he's known all along, and now my son is with him right now."

"I see. May I pray for him?"

"Um…sure. That would probably be great."

Marcus reached his hand out, but Rafe wasn't sure why. Slowly, he reached out as well, and Marcus took his hand in his. Rafe realized Marcus meant to pray for Grady right then and there. No one had ever asked to pray in front of him. Sure, there were people who said they prayed or would pray. Whether they did, Rafe had no idea.

"Father God in heaven, we come to You tonight in need. Rafe's son, Grady, needs Your help. He has entered a dark place where the people there don't care about him. They will use him and hurt him, and so we ask that You stand in their way. We ask that You block any weapon against him. We ask for protection around him. I also lift up Vera and thank You for bringing her to us. Having a federal agent involved will only make what we have to do easier. And finally, Lord, I ask that You touch Rafe in the place he hurts, where only Your healing hand can reach, and in the place that opens his heart to receive Your son Jesus. Show him, Father, that he is loved by You. That he always has been."

Rafe shook his head, refusing to let those words in. He pulled his hand, but Marcus held tight.

"It's true, Rafe. You are loved by the Creator of the universe. You are seen, and you are loved. And so is your son."

"I know he is," Rafe said. That he could believe.

"If you believe it for Grady, then why can't you believe it for yourself?"

Rafe watched a drop of water fall on his black pants. He sniffed and realized she was crying. He lifted his gaze to find not only Marcus watching him, but also Vera and Chris behind him. Chris had tears streaming down her face as she nodded.

"He does love you," she said. "So much."

"I don't know why." Rafe swiped at his eyes, forcing himself to stop. "I treat people horribly." He looked at Vera. "You should run away from me as fast as you can. Your file told you that."

Suddenly, she was beside him, looping her arm through his and swiping at his cheeks. "No. My file was all wrong. It missed so many details about you. It missed your unselfish love for your son. It missed how you put yourself on the back burner for him every day of your life. It missed how you chose loneliness to keep people safe. All the things you have done in secret have not been a secret to God. He has seen every single one. He does see you, and He does love you. And so do..."

Rafe locked his gaze onto Vera's. He realized his hand was free. Marcus had let go at some point. Rafe reached for Vera's cheek as Marcus stood and quietly disappeared down the hall with Chris.

"You love me?" he asked through a throat clogged with tears. Could he believe that, too?

"I shouldn't. I don't know how I would survive if Rossi took you as well. The fear that it will hurt more than losing my parents is real. But it doesn't change my feelings. So yes, Rafe, I do love you. All the reasons I stated that God loves you were actually why I love you. I'm not too well-versed when it comes to Bible teaching, but I can tell you this. God loves us regardless of the things that we have done or haven't done. His love is unconditional, and it has nothing to do with being worthy or not."

Rafe leaned back on the sofa with a heavy sigh. "I think I understand that. If I wasn't a father myself, I might not. But it's because of Grady and how I have loved him from afar that I think I do. I would do anything for him. Even if he joins the mob and takes over Rossi's organization, I will still love him, no matter what."

"Then how much more would our Father in heaven love us? And if he can fight for us, then I will fight for you."

"Really?" The impact of her words nearly knocked him over. She was willing to face her fear for him. But could he face his fear for her? His belief that she would leave like everyone else still felt so real.

"Yes. I want to try to give it my best, but I know it will mean believing that God will help me. I'll need His strength and His wisdom to keep you safe. I've tried to do this job without Him, and I can't anymore. And if Rossi does take you from me, then I will definitely need His comfort to get through it."

"I think I will need all of those things, too." He laughed nervously.

Vera smiled so brightly that her eyes lit up. He could see the love in her eyes…for him. She glanced at his lips and back at his eyes and back at his lips again. He wanted nothing more than to take her in his arms and kiss her, but he wanted this to be different than all the other women.

"I want to...cherish you," he said. "But I really want to kiss you, too."

"You can do both. I believe it's possible. Kiss me, Rafe. And make me feel cherished."

Rafe cupped her cheek and brought his lips to hers ever so gently. Just the simple touch of where they connected sent a shiver through his entire body. No one had ever made him feel so alive. It took a moment to grow used to the strange feeling coursing through him. She'd asked that he make her feel cherished, but he wasn't expecting her to do the same. And as she deepened the kiss, he never felt so loved. He felt himself changing with each sweet moment that passed by. He felt himself strengthening and becoming willing to fight his fear... for her.

Is that what love did? Did being loved fill him with strength and power so he could use it for good? *But what if I fail?*

Rafe pulled away, stunned at where his thoughts were heading. "I'm sorry," he said on a rush of air.

"Is something wrong?" Vera looked just as stunned.

"No." He needed to assure her. "Everything is... just right. But I'm still scared. I'm sorry." Rafe jumped to his feet and ran his fingers through his hair. He felt like his tie was still choking him, but he no longer wore it. "I'm going to hold you back. If anything happens to me, it won't be your fault. It will be my own. I need to be honest. I'm a cook. You're an agent. You can take down grown men with your bare hands. What can I offer you out there? A soufflé?"

Vera's eyes flashed with sadness. Or was it pity?

"I see." She stood and faced him head on. "The only thing I was asking for was your love, Rafe. But why should I be any different from any of the others you couldn't love, either?"

"But you *are* different. That's why I'm more scared than ever."

Vera frowned and turned for the hallway. "You're not scared of being in love, Rafe. You're afraid of making room in your life for someone else. Too many cooks in the kitchen."

CHRISTMAS EVE MORNING began with a snowstorm so strong that Vera wondered if she could carry out the plan that she and Marcus put together the days before. It had been six days since she shared that sweet kiss with Rafe, and since then he'd kept his distance from her and the planning.

"The snow is supposed to stop shortly," Chris said. "It's cold out there, but people will still be out and about doing their last-minute Christmas shopping. I say we move forward with the plan."

Vera looked at Rafe in the kitchen. He barely left the room since they arrived at the apartment. He said feeding people was the only thing he knew how to do, and he would stick to that. But instead of his delicious meals bringing them together, they felt like they only put a wedge between them. Every bite that excited all her senses only made her feel guilty if she said so. Yes, he was a terrific chef, but she disagreed that cooking was all that he was. If the only time she commended him for his work was for cooking, then she solidified his belief.

"What do you think, Rafe?" Vera asked. "Do I move forward with the plan? Or will Gus recognize me?"

He stood at the stove and flipped the eggs. "He won't recognize you. You look nothing like Roxie. You'll be great. You always are."

They were all compliments, but they fell flat knowing they came from his disappointment in himself.

Vera forced a smile and said to Marcus, "You'll be acting as my manager. Are you sure he's expecting me at noon?"

"Yes. And while you perform, I'll be looking around for any signs of their New Year's Eve plan."

"Then I guess everything is all set. We'll head to Creare right after breakfast."

Something crashed in the kitchen, and those sitting at the table pressed their lips together to refrain from saying anything. Rafe had lost a lot in the last couple of weeks. Vera couldn't make any promises that he would get his restaurant back. If he signed any kind of contract that gave the Vargas family control over the restaurant, that was outside her ability to fix.

"Sorry about that," Rafe said, carrying a tray of food to the table. "I dropped something."

"Not a problem," Chris said. "It happens to all of us. I do hope you're going to join us this morning."

Vera felt Rafe watching her as though she needed to give her permission. "Yes, I do hope you will, too," she said. She kicked the leg of the chair next to her to push the seat out. Thankfully, he took it, and she found herself closer to him than she had been for days.

Marcus led a prayer of thanks, but after he

finished, everyone sat still, feeling unsure what to say or do next. Did they talk about the plan in front of him after he had made it clear he felt useless to them?

"Well, don't just sit there. Eat. It's getting cold, and that's the worst thing you can do to a chef." Rafe cracked a smile. Instantly, the tension in the room released, and Chris let out a deep sigh.

"I think that's the longest you've been that moody. Are you good?" Chris looked at Vera. "Warning to you. When Rafe gets into one of his moods, watch out. It's even worse if he has his knife in his hand."

"Where is my knife?" Rafe sent raised eyebrows Vera's way.

"You'll get it back when the coast is clear. I thought it best to clean it up and hide it for a while. It's unique looking, and I'm sure Vic gave a detailed account of it."

"Thanks," Rafe said. He took a bite, and soon they were all digging in. They would need their strength for the day. And if all went as planned, it would be a long one.

"Anything I should know about Gus's taste in music? I need to wow him immediately." Vera waited for Rafe to finish chewing.

He picked up his napkin and wiped the corners of his mouth. "As beautiful as your arias are, stick to more show tunes and Christmas music. Those are more up the alley of the Vargas family businesses."

"I can do that," Vera said. "I wish you could come." There, she said what was on her mind. "I hate doing this without you."

"He'll recognize me. I don't think there's any costume out there that would hide my identity from Gus. Not even a Santa suit."

Vera giggled at the thought. Then she sobered. "Why not?"

Rafe's eyes bugged out. "No way am I dressing up as Santa Claus. You can forget about it."

Vera grabbed his hand beside hers. "Hear me out. We could take a page from Nico Rossi's playbook. He had one of his men standing guard around the corner of Creare. He was dressed as Santa and ringing a bell, supposedly for donations. But probably to watch the restaurant."

"No, he was too far away for that," Rafe replied, sitting straighter in the chair. "But what if he was positioned there for a different reason? What if he was there to scope out Nico's next heist?"

"Yes!" Vera jumped to her feet and ran to her bag on the couch. She retrieved the phone and brought up the map again. Marcus moved his chair closer as Rafe stood beside her.

"There." She pointed to where the goon had tripped her. It was less than a mile away from the restaurant, and it was in a perfect diagonal line to Creare.

Marcus pulled the location up on his phone. "It's a post office building. Bearer Bonds, maybe? Seems like a waste of C-4, though."

Rafe asked, "What's across the street?"

Marcus moved the screen. "A bank. Much more promising. All right, let me put some feelers out to the coalition. Maybe someone knows something about this bank and its affiliations with the mob. I'll be right back." Marcus disappeared down the hall, making his first call to someone in his group. He closed the door to the bedroom, leaving the three of them to complete the plan.

"How fast can we get a Santa costume?" Vera asked Chris.

Chris smiled. "How about less than an hour? I'm sure some of my old friends from the stage will have a connection to that. Let me make that call." She, too, disappeared down the hall on her mission, leaving Vera alone with Rafe.

Both sat in their chairs, staring at each other.

Vera reached for his hand, sighing at how good it felt to touch him again. "What was that about you only being good enough for cooking? Because from what I just watched, you may have cracked this entire case wide open."

"Would it be inappropriate for me to say I may still dream about that day?"

Vera squinted in confusion. "What day?"

"The day you took Santa down. I think that was the moment I started to fall for you."

Vera touched her cheek. By the scorching feel, she was pretty sure she was bright pink. "So, you admit to falling for me, huh?"

"I figured that was old news. Did I not say so?" His slight smile curled her toes.

Vera shook her head. "No, you did not. You just let me confess my heart."

Rafe reached for her cheek, cupping the back of her head. He brought his forehead close to hers, so they touched. "I really am a jerk. I warned you."

"I missed you," Vera whispered. "This last week has been…horrible."

"I missed you more. I made you all my favorite meals just so I could watch you enjoy them." He squeezed his eyes shut. "I know. Silly." He peeked out from one eye.

Vera laughed, loving his cuteness. "I didn't want to say anything, but wow, Rafe. I almost cried a few times. They were so good. You are amazing."

"Not as amazing as you." He tilted his head and whispered, "I love you, Vera."

Vera thought her cheeks split open with the smile she couldn't contain. "I love you, too."

"You know what I'm going to miss most today?"

She shook her head. "What?"

"Hearing you sing when you go to audition at Creare. I'll be freezing on the street in a Santa costume while Gus gets to listen to your beautiful voice."

"I can sing just for you anytime."

"I'm holding you to it."

Vera thought of the plan, now including Rafe, and grew worried. She had been fine with the setup when he would remain here at Chris's apartment. But now, he would be out on the street, keeping watch.

"You have to wear the wire again, okay? And I'll give you your knife back," she said. "If anything appears out of the ordinary, you get out of there. Promise?"

"I'll be fine."

"Promise me, Rafe."

He smiled and pressed a kiss on her lips. "I promise."

"No saving me."

"That I can't promise." He kissed her again. "Don't make me, please."

Vera relaxed and sighed into his embrace, enjoying the feel of him all round her. "Okay." She kissed him back. She loved his lips. She may love his kisses almost as much as she loved him.

"Oh! I'm so sorry!" Chris spoke loudly from the hallway.

Vera pulled back on a gasp. Over Rafe's shoulder, she saw the smile on Chris's face, which said she was not sorry in the least.

"No, you're not," Vera accused her.

Chris laughed. "Nope. Not at all."

Marcus stood beside his wife, looking much more serious. "We need to talk," he said.

Rafe turned around as the room grew quiet. "What did you find out?"

"I know what they're after. Gold bars. And a lot of them." Marcus approached the table and took the seat at the head. He folded his hands on the tabletop. "An order from a bank in Singapore was placed by an importer here in the city. It is due to arrive on New Year's Eve by 5:00 p.m. It will arrive by plane at

Kennedy and be brought by an armored car to this very bank near Creare. It will be transported to the vault until the importer arrives Saturday to pick it up."

Vera sat back and crossed her arms. "But if there should be an explosion to take out that whole mile block before New Year's Eve strikes, all that might be left is a vault with gold bars."

Marcus said, "Exactly. The devastation would pull all emergency personnel to helping the victims. It will be gold bars for the taking. Rossi's got plenty of men who can crack a safe. This will probably be Rossi's easiest heist yet."

"Most profitable," Rafe said.

"Most destructive," Vera added, thinking of that woman who died at the last one. Vera stood from her chair, now more determined than ever to stop Rossi. "Let's get this show on the road, folks. My hands are itching to cuff someone before the night is out."

CHAPTER 11

*V*era left Rafe in his Santa suit out in front of the restaurant. She entered the building with Marcus and Chris, but with the restaurant not opened yet, she found the dining room empty. She hoped the dim light would shield her face from Gus, and he wouldn't recognize Roxie in her.

"Hold on. I'll check the kitchen," Chris said, heading to the swinging doors. "I may not own the place anymore, but I know my way around. I'll tell Gus I have a brilliant singer for him to hear, and I'll try to hold back my two cents about his sneaky small print."

Vera headed to the stage where Roxie Moon had sung her heart out only a few weeks ago. So much had happened since she pushed her way into Rafe's life, nearly breaking his nose. She glanced out the window to see him ringing the bell, wanting to keep him in her sights just in case something went down. As she stepped up on the stage, she realized there wasn't much room to sing up there anymore. A huge Christmas tree had been erected in the middle. Numerous Christmas presents were piled beneath it and around it, barely leaving any room to stand.

"Maybe this won't work after all," she whispered to Marcus. "If he put the tree here, maybe he's not hiring talent anymore."

"He said to come in for an audition. Let's stick with the plan." Marcus replied, but after another 10 minutes with no sign of Chris or Gus, Vera knew something was up.

"I think we abort," she whispered.

Marcus headed to the doors. "Not without Chris."

Vera moved to go after him, but she also didn't want to take her eyes off Rafe. If something was going down, he had no protection out there. This was turning into a nightmare. *Why did I let him do this?*

A knot formed in Vera's throat, tightening, while the corner of her eyes burned from keeping them wide open. She didn't dare blink for what might happen in that split second.

Then her gaze fell on the presents.

Could it be? Were these the same presents from the gala? The very ones she saw being taken out the front door and loaded onto the truck? They were all gold and silver wrapped just like the gifts at the event.

Vera approached the stage again, but this time, she reached the gift closest to her. She tore at the paper, the sound like the slash of a knife.

"Vera, stop right there," a familiar voice spoke from behind. "You don't want to do that."

Without turning around, Vera knew her handler stood behind her. What excuse would Tangen give her? That he had taken over the investigation and was undercover? Three weeks ago, she would have bought that line without a second thought.

Instead of turning around, Vera continued to rip the paper away.

"Vera. Don't."

But she kept ripping, already filling her fists with paper as she ripped the last piece off and lifted the cover.

Just the sight of the C-4 stalled her breath. The solid, dirty-white material with a putty like texture looked like modeling clay but had a distinct smell of motor oil. Every gift in front of her had smuggled in this explosive. They most likely had been brought to the gala to transfer to Rossi without anyone the wiser. To all the guests, it looked like he was being showered with presents. It now was in place for their grand finale.

Slowly, she turned to face her handler. "You never had any intention of letting me arrest Rossi, did you? You sent me on one wild goose chase after another."

"I always kept you one step away."

Her throat made a guttural sound. "Your partner, the one you claimed, went to the dark side...that was you all along." She remembered coming on to the Bureau and him seeking her out. "You claimed we had the same vendetta. You played on my pain and convinced me to work with you to catch him."

Vera fisted her hands at her sides.

"You will never catch him. I do have to admit, when you disappeared, I got nervous. But I know you better than you know yourself. I knew you would be back because cuffing Rossi is the only thing you live for."

Tangen moved slowly toward her. She saw the

needle in his hand and figured Marcus and Chris had already succumbed to the injection.

"You're despicable," she said.

"I'm rich. Filthy rich." Tangen waved to the presents. "And after this week, even more so. I would say I don't have to work another day in my life, but I like what I do."

"Pretending to be an agent, you mean?"

"It has its perks. I'm always in the know, and that keeps my clients happy." He picked up his steps and moved the hand with the needle above his head.

Vera grabbed hold of his wrist and held it high while her other hand punched straight into his solar plexus. With her right foot, she swept out and brought him to his knees.

Tangen laughed up at her. "I taught you well." His smile fell from his face and his lips sneered. "I knew you would do that. Just like I know you'll do this." He grabbed her leg and pulled her down, and just as he did, she wrapped his head between her knees and twisted to her side.

She knew instantly that he let her do that. She was falling right into his hands like the putty in the C-4.

Tangen had molded her into the agent she was.

She was his creation, and he knew every move she would make.

Except for one.

He believed she would always choose the job over love. That's how he made sure he had full control of her. When she went rogue, she became a liability to him.

This battle would only end in death. As she held his head between her legs and his hand in hers, she realized he still had a free hand. At any second, she expected to be stabbed in the back. Inhaling deep within her, Vera opened her mouth and let out the highest note she'd ever sang. She was sure people over a block heard her voice. She knew Rafe did. But would he come help her? She had asked him not to try to save her again. In this moment, she knew that had been wrong of her to demand that of him. He had every right to want to love and protect her as she did him.

But would he comply and not come to help her out of respect for her wishes?

Suddenly an arm circled Tangen's neck. He screamed in pain as he was lifted from her. Vera flipped him over onto his back as Rafe's black booted foot slammed on her handler's back. She reached into Tangen's pocket and took out his own handcuffs to use on him.

"Call 911. Chris and Marcus need an ambulance immediately. And I need the police to take this dirty agent away." Vera remained in position while Rafe used the phone at the host desk to make the call.

"They're on their way. Do you need help?" he asked.

She smiled at him. "No, but I take back what I said. You can save me anytime. I've got him. Go help Chris and Marcus." Rafe hesitated, tearing his fake beard from his face. "Go!"

He ran back to the kitchen, busting through both swinging doors. A minute went by, and she heard nothing.

"Rafe! Talk to me! What's going on?" Vera called out.

No response.

"Rafe?" Vera called again.

Still nothing.

Beneath her, Tangen's shoulders shook with quiet laughter. "That was too easy. You're alone, my dear. You might as well give up. You were never going to win this."

"Who's back there? Is it Gus? What have you done with them?" Vera shook Tangen, demanding an answer. Did she let her handler go to help the others?

Vera didn't know what to do. All she knew was Rafe had just walked into a trap.

And she sent him into it.

RAFE SHIVERED, and his teeth chattered, sending pain up into his head. Or was the pain from something else? Reaching up, his trembling hands touched a sticky substance on the side of his temple. A vague memory of something black flying toward him surfaced. He'd been hit. By a pan.

But by whom?

And where was he now?

Rafe forced his eyes open but was only met with more darkness. Cold and black. *No*. Freezing was more like it.

On his back, he stared upward as his hands felt around him, touching what felt like a tiled floor. He rolled to his right and reached farther. He met nothing but air. To his left, his hand made contact with something unmovable. Feeling his way, he touched something soft…something like…*lips*? His mind registered that he was touching a face.

Rafe pulled back on a gasp, realizing a person lied beside him.

He wasn't alone.

But how many more were there? Were they lined up in here like sardines in a can?

And where was here?

Rafe sat up and pulled on his other senses. He inhaled deeply and instantly knew where he was.

My freezer.

Whoever hit him stuffed him inside the walk-in freezer to die. Leaning back to the body beside him, he shook it. Feeling the face again, he touched long hair. "Chris? Is that you? Wake up."

Getting to his knees, he reached down under her armpits to lift her up and shake her. She hung like a lifeless rag doll. He brought her down gently and felt beside her.

Another body that could only be Marcus.

"Marcus!" Rafe shouted, grabbing hold of his limp hand and shaking it. "Wake up!"

Rafe went for their necks. *Please, be alive.* "Please, God!"

His trembling fingers searched on their skin for anything to tell him they were alive. He found nothing. But his fingers were so numb. Maybe he was missing it. He felt their heads but found no blood. They weren't hit like he was.

Gunshots?

Again, he felt every place on them, even rolling them over for any sign of blood. He found nothing. He wondered how long it took someone to freeze to death. They couldn't have been in here that much longer than him. Were they poisoned? It wouldn't be the first time someone was poisoned at his restaurant, but this would have been instant.

Rafe needed to get them out of there. If they were still alive, it wouldn't be for much longer.

His walk-in had two sections. The first section was a refrigerator. Inside that was the entrance to the freezer, where they had been put…by someone.

Standing, Rafe felt his way to the door and found the emergency release. He pulled it, and the door swung inward. He felt for a box on the shelf and brought it down to prop the door open.

Returning to the freezer, he lifted Chris from under her arms and dragged her into the refrigerator. Letting her down gently, he returned, feeling his way to Marcus, and did the same before shutting the freezer door.

Now for the refrigerator door.

But would that someone be waiting on the other

side? Maybe they didn't realize there were emergency releases on the off chance someone locked himself on the inside. Maybe they weren't guarding the door and had just left them for dead.

"Rafe!" a faint familiar voice called from the other side.

Vera.

But was it another trap? Was she being held on the other side?

Suddenly, the door swung open, and there she was with two police officers behind her. She reached for him at the same time he pulled her into his arms.

"Is the ambulance here? I don't know if they're alive." He returned to lift Chris out of the refrigerator. The two police officers retrieved Marcus.

Vera said, "They were injected with something. I don't know what it was. I gave the syringe to the paramedics."

"And that man? Who was that?"

"Tangen, my handler." She frowned. "I had to let him go."

"Let him go? Why?"

"I had to make the choice. It was you or him. I chose you."

"Which way did he go?"

"Out the front."

"But someone hit me in the kitchen. Where did that person go?"

Vera looked to the back door, the only other exit. She took off, bursting through the exit with Rafe on her heels.

"Stay with the police!" she ordered.

"No way am I leaving your side again!"

They raced around the back and to the front of the restaurant, stopping at the street to look both ways.

"There!" Vera shouted and took off running again.

Three blocks down, Rafe spotted Tangen, still cuffed with his hands behind his back, turn the corner. He followed Vera, but spotted Marcus's car. Marcus had given him the keys just in case he had to make a run for it.

Rafe jumped in behind the wheel and started the engine. Vera kept running faster than he had ever seen her. But not as fast as a car. He pulled up beside her, leaning over to push the passenger door wide. "Get in!"

She leaped inside and slammed the door as he took off. "Take a right!" She rolled the window down.

"I saw where he went," Rafe assured her, noticing she already held her gun in her hand.

"Are you going to shoot him?"

"If I have to." She didn't sound too excited about the idea.

"I'm sorry," Rafe said, knowing what this man meant to her. Without her parents, Tangen had become a father figure.

She shrugged. "I'll get over it. Especially after he's in custody."

Rafe dodged the Christmas Eve traffic, weaving in and out of taxicabs, keeping his eyes trained on the dirty agent. A car pulled up to him, and the door opened for him. Tangen jumped into the passenger side as the car drove off. Rafe recognized the vehicle immediately.

Rafe slammed the steering wheel, feeling the gut punch. "Gus."

"Are you sure? Could be someone driving his car."

Rafe smiled at her. "Thanks for trying to make me feel better, but we both know it's him. We both know he hit me over the head, and now he's rescuing Tangen."

"Stay on them. They can't drive forever. This is

New York City. They're bound to get stopped in their tracks."

"On it," Rafe mumbled, swerving around a fire truck that was entering the road. The little rental handled surprisingly well in this emergency. "Get ready to jump out if you have to."

Snowflakes hit the windshield and Rafe flipped the wipers on as he sped up. A taxi cut in front of him, but he swerved around it just in time to see Gus's car turn right.

"Be careful. He could be leading you," Vera warned.

"To where?"

"Beats me. Maybe right off a bridge. Just be careful."

"Can you shoot out the tires or something?"

"You would have to get closer. I can't just shoot in a city with people all around. That would be highly irresponsible of me."

Then Rafe would get her closer. He hit the pedal to the floor, speed climbing to 102 mph. The gap lessened between them, and suddenly Gus stopped.

Rafe hit the brakes, screeching along the icy roads. He turned the wheel as his front end nearly hit the rear of the car head-on. The back of the car slammed into Gus's before Gus took off again.

Rafe hit the gas pedal, straightening out the steering wheel. But the car had been compromised. He gritted his teeth as he pushed it to its limits to continue the chase.

Suddenly, Gus's car cut right so sharply that it lifted on two wheels. He drove down an alley that extended through the block. Rafe followed, hitting trash cans along the way. He could only hope no one would step out of their back entrances. Gus burst out onto a street and crossed through traffic to enter another alley. Rafe nearly lost him when a truck pulled in front of him. He quickly maneuvered and caught up, once again, back in a long alley. The next street, Gus came to a complete stop.

A barricade had been set up for the Christmas Day Parade the next morning. Police cars lined the street, and officers came out to see what was going on.

Rafe stopped inches from his car as Vera jumped out. "FBI! Hands where I can see them!"

She approached the passenger side of the vehicle and yanked the door wide. With her gun in one hand, she reached in and grabbed the back of Tangen's coat, pulling him out onto the ground, none too gently. Rafe could see the handcuffs were still on the man. Assured that Vera had it covered, he raced to the driver's door. All he could see was the shadow of someone's hands up above their head. He just might remove Gus the same way, he thought.

Except, when Rafe pulled the door wide, it wasn't Gus driving.

"We meet again," Rafe said, staring at the man who nearly killed him in the last alley.

Vic Simons.

Rafe reached into his coat and withdrew his knife. "Remember this? I suggest you do as you're told, or you'll see how good I am with it again."

Three officers approached with their guns drawn. "Drop your weapon, Santa!"

"It's not a weapon. It's my cooking knife. I was just showing it to him."

"He's with me," Vera said. "Arrest these men for trying to blow up the city. There are cops over at Creare right now with fifty pounds of C-4, planted by these two."

"I heard the call," one of the police officers said. "Good work, agent, catching them. You saved a lot of lives today."

An officer lifted Tangen from the ground and stuffed him in the back of the cruiser. All the while, the dirty cop cried that he wanted his lawyer. Vic went quietly to his own cruiser as Rafe and Vera stared at each other over the hood of the car. He knew what she was thinking. These were not the arrests she wanted. There was no way either of those men were going to squawk about Nico Rossi's part in the plan. Once again, the mobster went free.

The car made a sound like someone knocked on it. Then it did it again, coming from the back.

"Stop," Vera said, holding her gun up. She nodded for Rafe to stay at the front of the car. "Pop the trunk," she whispered.

Rafe nodded and reached inside the car to pull the lever. The trunk opened, and immediately they could hear someone mumbling.

Vera crept alongside the vehicle until she could peek in. She waved for officers to come back and two of them ran up beside her with their guns drawn.

"Rafe? You're going to want to see this," Vera said as she stood at the end of the car. "Someone, get an ambulance. Fast."

Whatever it was, it was bad. Vera's face had blanched. Rafe raced to the back of the car and, even through all the blood, he knew who it was.

"Oh, Gus. No." Rafe reached in to lift his friend's head. "What did they do to you?"

"I didn't know...I'm...sorry," Gus gurgled

through blood. Before he could say anything else, his eyes closed as paramedics stepped in to lift him from the car. They placed him on a stretcher and whisked him into the back of an ambulance.

Rafe looked back at Vera, uncertain of what to do. She nodded. "Go. Be with him."

The way she said it, she didn't believe he was long for this world. Rafe ran up into the vehicle right before the doors closed. He watched her grow smaller as the ambulance raced down the street, unobstructed by any vehicles, with a clear path to the hospital.

"Rafe...Rafe," Gus whispered.

"I'm right here, Gumbo." Rafe touched his bloodied hand and held it tight.

"Rossi...he wanted me to ruin you. He threatened my father. I thought..." Gus swallowed hard. "I thought I could help instead and save Creare. But then those two showed up and planned to blow the place up."

"I know. But you're sure Nico Rossi put you up to ruining me?"

Gus nodded before his eyes closed once again.

There wouldn't be proof that Rossi had anything to do with the explosives, but would there be enough evidence to put him away for extortion? At least for a few years?

When Rafe reached the hospital, Vera was waiting for him after arriving in a police cruiser. They stood together with their arms clasped around each other as Gus was wheeled into surgery. Vera approached the desk.

"I need to know about the two others that were brought in here who were unconscious," she spoke to the nurse. "I'm FBI."

"Right this way," the nurse said, standing and leading them to the back. "They're both awake but still groggy. Thankfully, the doctors knew what they were injected with and could combat it with the right protocol. They'll both be okay." She held the door wide. "But be quick."

Rafe let Vera enter first and followed from behind. Chris and Marcus were in their own beds beside each other but holding hands in the gap.

"Is it over?" Chris asked.

Vera replied, "Yes. At least for me it is."

"What? What are you talking about?" Rafe asked her. "You haven't cuffed Nico Rossi yet. You can't back down now. You can get him on *something*."

Vera stepped up to him and took his face in her hands. "You once asked me if I would choose cuffing

Nico Rossi over love, and I said cuffing him. But I was wrong, Rafe. I choose love. It's time to let it go."

"But will he let you go?"

Vera smiled. "I said I would choose love and stop chasing him down. I didn't say I wouldn't be ready to arrest him if the opportunity arose. But after today, I have a feeling he's going to leave me alone for a little while. He knows he's being watched, and he's lost his man inside the Bureau to protect him. He'll lie low. He also has Grady now. Sadly, the boy will be Rossi's focus for the time being."

Rafe saw the sympathy in her eyes, and he was glad he wasn't facing this loss alone. "Yeah, Rossi has years to make up for teaching Grady his evil ways. Rossi also knows he hurts me every day with that knowledge. Killing me now would take away that joy."

"Then we wait. Together." A soft smile flitted across of her lips. "What do you say? Is there room for two in your kitchen?"

Rafe laughed. "I promise to never kick you out again."

Her smile fell from her face. She locked her gaze on his, capturing him fully. "And I promise to never leave."

Hearing those words brought tears to his eyes.

With a laugh of pure joy in the back of his throat, Rafe felt a little lightheaded. He imagined this would be the type of life he had with Vera Sharp. He expected whiplash at every turn and looked forward to it.

"I love you," he said. "I really, really love you and I trust you."

Tears filled her eyes and spilled onto her cheeks. "If Rossi ever comes for you, I won't cuff him. I will *gut* him."

Rafe laughed a little uneasily. "Does that mean you love me too?"

"Oh, yeah. And I don't care who knows."

Rafe leaned down and kissed her fully. He breathed in this powerful but yet sweet woman. It bowled him over that she was his and he was hers.

Forever more.

The clock neared midnight on New Year's Eve. Creare was jampacked with customers, ready to count down. New York City on New Year's Eve held a life of its own. So much energy flowed through the streets and the restaurants. Times Square squished as many people in as possible. But here at the restaurant, Rafe and Vera sat on the stage with their closest friends, with the window behind them, giving them the best of view of the fireworks ready to go off.

Mel and Jeremy sat together across the table. Baby Joey bounced on his dad's knee. Chris and Marcus huddled together beside them, whispering and pointing at the baby. Rafe wondered if they were considering starting a family yet. He'd wait to ask at another time. He thought of his own son and tried to push away his melancholy. Rafe had missed so much, and now, with his son estranged, he would miss so much more.

"I heard from the Andrews," he said. "Grady arrived in North Carolina yesterday. He's back, but they said he won't talk to them either."

The frowns of his friends gave him peace that he didn't have to go through this alone.

"I'll be praying for him every day," Mel said. "I'll be praying that he doesn't reject God's help."

Vera squeezed Rafe's hand. "Me too. And for you too."

Rafe hung his head. "I understand God's love now. I've made room for Him in my life too. But I know Grady won't accept God's help until he knows he's loved by Him. So please pray for that. Pray that Grady knows God loves him."

Vera rested her head on Rafe's shoulder. She sighed. "It really has made all the difference, hasn't it?"

Rafe nodded and kissed the top of her head. "Like night and day."

Mel grinned his way. "I've never seen you so at peace, Rafe. I don't think I've heard you yell at anyone since we arrived yesterday. Even when the new chef spilled your sauce everywhere. That took some patience on your part." She winked at Vera.

Rafe growled, feigning his annoyance. Sort of.

People stood from their chairs and approach the windows. The countdown was about to begin. Couples embraced each other as they prepared to watch the fireworks.

"I wish Gus was here," Rafe whispered into Vera's ear.

"He's going to be okay. Give him time. He feels guilty."

"But I told him I forgive him."

"He needs to forgive himself now." Vera stood and took his hand to lead him to the window. She leaned up and kissed him sweetly on the lips. "Have I told you how much I love you today?" she whispered.

"Yes, but you can tell me again." He smiled down at her. "Happy New Year, my love. I feel it's going to be a great one."

"Magical."

"Hey, you guys we need to do this more often," Mel said. She looped her arm through Chris's and pulled her close to the window.

Chris said, "I say every year at Creare for New Year's."

Mel nodded enthusiastically. "And July 4th in Connecticut at our place. There's enough room for everybody. The house is huge." She elbowed her husband, who was now building something else on the property. Jeremy couldn't keep his hands still.

"Spring and fall in Savannah are beautiful," Chris said. "Just saying."

They all nodded in agreement and pledged to make getting together an effort.

"Ten, nine, eight…" The crowd in the restaurant grew louder and rowdier. "Seven, six, five, four…"

Vera turned her face toward Rafe, and he breathed her in as they both finished the countdown together. "Three, two, one." Their lips found each other's.

The noise in the restaurant died down as couples leaned close to their loved ones. Rafe would never take for granted this moment.

Suddenly, the room erupted into cheers. The new year had been welcomed in enthusiastically. They all stared out to watch the fireworks explode into vibrant color in the skies.

Then Rafe said, "Am I the only one holding my breath?"

Slowly, each of them nodded and agreed. Mel said, "Yeah, I was hoping one of those C-4 explosives didn't get left behind in here. I was trusting that you guys got rid of it all."

They all laughed but maybe a bit uneasily.

Vera said, "Rossi has been stopped."

They all replied in unison, "For now."

A NOTE FROM KATY

Thank you reading *Real Cold*. Vera and Rafe were a lot of fun to write about. Are you wondering what happened to Grady? Find out in Two Wrongs to Right part of the Royal Bay Beach Club series. Don't forget to grab the prequel Table for One for free at KatyLeeBooks.com

FREE SHORT STORY!

Sign up for more book updates and my monthly "Novel Ideas" Newsletter that goes out every full moon and receive a **FREE** short story ebook here: www.katyleebooks.com

Table for One is the prequel to the up-and-coming Royal Bay Billionaire Beach Club, where money can lead to love...or murder...or both.

Happy Reading!
   Katy

Left at the altar may just be the best thing that's ever happened to her.

Becca Shane has a cruise to catch, even if she's now boarding her honeymoon solo.

Patrick Joyce has a daughter to raise after his wife turned her back on him when he needed her the most.

Neither believe in love, but can they believe in each other?

OTHER BOOKS BY KATY LEE

All books can be ordered through KatyLeeBooks.com

§⟲

Real Virtue

Book One in the Web of Lies series

In a virtual reality game where she can fly, someone's aiming to take her down.

Mel Mesini is a New York City restaurateur and an avid virtual reality world traveler. She's risen above her misfit life and now bears a striking resemblance to her glamorous gaming avatar. But her successful life-both online and in reality-takes a swerve the night her father is seriously injured in a hit-and-run. Mel is careened back to her judgmental hometown, where being the daughter of the town's crazy lady had made her an outcast. To make matters worse, Officer Jeremy Stiles, the man whose harsh, rejecting words had cut her the deepest, is heading the investigation.

Jeremy knows he hurt Mel and attempts to make amends by finding her father's assailant. When he realizes she's the actual target, his plan for reconciliation turns to one of protection-whether she wants his help or not. What he wants are answers, especially about this online game she plays. Is it a harmless *pastime*, as she says? Or is she using it to cover something up? As a faceless predator destroys the things that matter to her, Jeremy knows he's running out of time before she loses the one thing that matters most-her real life.

Real Justice

Book Two in the Web of Lies series

A ransom note left in her apartment tells Christina Depalo that changing her name and hiding in the big city hadn't been enough to escape her dangerous family. The Morans have kidnapped her roommate, demanding Christina return to Georgia. But that will mean facing the cutthroat attorney Marcus Cartwright, a man she once loved but who only wanted to take down her family.

Marcus had started a coalition with his friend to crack down on organized crime in Savannah. But when his friend loses his life in a supposed accident, nothing will stop Marcus from seeking justice, not even the Moran's prodigal daughter who left town twelve years ago. Nobody will derail him this time.

But then Christina never was a nobody.

Warning Signs

Stepping Stones Island Series Book 1

GUILTY UNTIL PROVEN INNOCENT

When a drug-smuggling ring rocks a small coastal town, the DEA sends Agent Owen Matthews to shut it down. A single father with a deaf son, Owen senses that the town's number one suspect—the high school's new principal—doesn't fit the profile. Miriam Hunter hoped to shrug off the stigma of her hearing impairment when she returned to Stepping Stones, Maine. But her recurring nightmares dredge up old memories that could prove her innocence—and uncover the truth behind a decades-old murder. Yet Owen's help may not be enough when someone decides to keep Miriam silenced—permanently.

Grave Danger

Stepping Stones Island series Book 2

BONES OF CONTENTION

When skeletal remains are found on a small Maine island, forensic anthropologist Lydia Muir is sent to investigate. It's Lydia's job to determine whether the homicide happened long ago—or more recently. Island sheriff Wesley Grant seems sure the murder didn't happen on *his* watch. But when Lydia uncovers the victim's identity, someone goes to great lengths to get Lydia off the island. Wes vows to protect her, but is the handsome lawman holding something back? To help catch a killer, she'll have to trust him—or become the next victim.

Sunken Treasure

Stepping Stones Island Series Book 3

DANGER ON THE HIGH SEAS

Shipwreck diver Gage Fontaine is used to modern-day pirates chasing after his boat and the buried treasure he salvages. But when he unknowingly leads a dangerous criminal to the waters off Stepping Stones Island, he puts a beautiful fisherwoman in grave danger. Rachelle Thibodaux has spent the past year hiding on her boat to avoid the town's censure for her father's crimes. But when she comes face-to-face with a gun-wielding pirate, she becomes a new kind of target. To save her own life, she'll have to work with Gage to find the treasure before the pirates do.

Permanent Vacancy

Stepping Stones Island Series Book 4

BUYER BEWARE

When Gretchen Bauer begins renovating an old Victorian house to turn it into a bed-and-breakfast, she barely escapes several dangerous "accidents" at her home. Colm McCrae, host of the home improvement TV show helping her renovate, refuses to believe these aren't on purpose. Could this be a harmful ploy by his boss to boost ratings? Yet with Colm's Irish brogue and handsome face, Gretchen wonders whether he could be involved. But with a whole town full of neighbors disgruntled about the inn bringing strangers to their shores, Gretchen has a list of more likely suspects. Now she must trust Colm if she wants to keep her new business venture from turning into a five-star death trap.

Silent Night Pursuit

Roads to Danger Series Book 1: Family secrets resurface

RACE AGAINST TIME

Lacey Phillips believes Captain Wade Spencer knows something about her brother's mysterious death. So she throws caution to the wind and tracks him down on

Christmas Eve looking for answers. Wade tries to turn her away—until bullets start to fly. He doesn't want to take the stubborn beauty on his life-or-death mission to find out the truth about how Wade's past may have cost her brother his life. But with killers lurking everywhere, he has to protect her—especially when she breaches the walls around his heart. Can Wade and his faithful service dog keep Lacey alive long enough to figure out who's targeting them?

Blindsided / Ransom Rescue

Roads to Danger Series Book 2: Family secrets resurface

UNDERCOVER RESCUE

When race-car track owner Veronica Spencer discovers stolen cars in a garage on her track, she knows she's been framed. But before Roni can do anything about it, the criminals kidnap her. Undercover FBI agent Ethan Gunn shouldn't break his cover to protect Roni, but he won't watch her die, either. Despite his FBI information that says she's involved in the crime ring, Ethan knows she's innocent. So he risks it all to help her break free. But now, with killers and the FBI on their trail, Ethan must find a way to keep her safe…and clear her name.

High Speed Holiday

Roads to Danger Series Book 3: Family secrets resurface

TANGLED PAST

After Ian Stone discovers he was kidnapped when he was a baby, he journeys to his "family's" hometown—and is shot at shortly after he arrives. Now he's convinced the Spencers don't want their long-lost brother, Luke, to return and claim his inheritance. But local chief of police Sylvie Laurent doesn't believe his siblings would try to kill him. And the stubborn woman is determined to protect him until she uncovers the truth. At first, Sylvie is skeptical of Ian's story…but he bears a strong resemblance to the Spencers. And they'll have to work together to stay ahead of the danger if they want to live to see him reunited with his family at Christmas.

Amish Country Undercover

Rogues Ridge Setting

Secrets, sabotage and small-town danger. *Someone wants an Amish woman dead.*

Taking the reins of her father's Amish horse-trading business, Grace Miller's prepared for backlash over breaking community norms—but not for sabotage. Now someone's willing to do anything it takes to make sure she fails, and it's undercover FBI agent Jack Kaufman's mission to stop them. But can Jack face his own Amish past long enough to shield Grace from a killer?

Amish Sanctuary
Rogues Ridge Setting

A woman on the run. A baby in danger. Can her Amish ex-fiancé save them?

To keep her patient's baby safe from a killer, counselor Naomi Kemp will do things she never thought possible, like return to her Amish hometown…and her ex-fiancé. Widower Sawyer Zook can offer Naomi and the baby protection and a place to hide. But Sawyer can't shield Naomi from what threatens her most: the traumatic past that drove her away years ago…

Framed in Amish Country: A Novella
Rogues Ridge Setting

Despite the disapproval of her Amish community, teacher Lizzie Fisher has fought for an independent life—even going so far as to tutor at the English school. Alex Wilson, a young English painter hired to paint the school, is used to being ridiculed because of his learning disabilities. He questions why the smart, pretty, Amish woman treats him differently. When Alex finds himself framed for a crime, he believes there is no hope for him, but Lizzie is sure her community will come to his aid. Except, their forbidden relationship may give Lizzie the independence she thought she always wanted.

Holiday Suspect Pursuit

Mysteries in New Mexico Series Book 1

Unraveling a murder mystery...could unlock his lost memories...

After a murderer strikes, former deputy Jett Butler and his search-and-rescue dog must work with the sole witness—FBI agent Nicole Harrington. But Nicole's the ex-fiancée he left behind after a car accident gave him amnesia years ago. And in a fight to survive the holidays, remembering his past might be just as dangerous as facing the killer on their heels...

Cavern Cover Up

Mysteries in New Mexico Series Book 2

A suspicion that her father's murder is linked to a smuggling ring sends private investigator Danika Lewis pursuing a lead all the way to Carlsbad Caverns National Park. Teaming up with ranger Tru Butler to search deep off-limits caves for the missing artifacts is the fastest way to uncover the truth. But there's danger in the dark and a killer on the loose who will do anything to keep secrets hidden.

§

Santa Fe Setup

Mysteries in New Mexico Series Book 3

Soon after artist Luci Butler learns someone's been hiding drugs *inside her paintings* she also discovers ruthless criminals are aiming to silence her. Only her brother's coworker, Bard Holland, is on her side. The pair must race to clear her name and track a murderer straight into the unforgiving mountains of New Mexico. Despite Bard's determined protection, Luci is being drawn dangerously close into a killer's merciless endgame.

§

Christmas K-9 Unit Heroes

Danger comes to Denver for the holidays in this Publisher's Weekly Bestseller.

The clock is ticking in Silent Night Explosion by Katy Lee - but can Jodie Chen trust the newest K-9 officer on the force, Victor Abrams, and his dog to find a bomb and keep her alive...despite Victor's shadowed past? And with veterinarian Sydney Jones being targeted, K-9 Officer Gavin Walker and his furry partner must stand between her and certain death in Lenora Worth's Hidden Christmas Danger.

K-9 National Park Defenders

A #1 Publisher's Weekly Bestseller!

Start making plans for a superb night, ushering in your holidays with these two riveting novellas!

A Christmas skiing retreat turns treacherous when Pacific Northwest K-9 Unit Officer Veronica Eastwood's sister is kidnapped in North Cascades National Park—and only rival Officer Parker Walsh can help her in Katy Lee's Yuletide Ransom. And in Sharee Stover's explosive Holiday Rescue Countdown, K-9 officers Dylan Jeong and Brandie Weller must race against the clock in Olympic National Park when they face a Christmas parade bomb threat...and a killer from Dylan's past.

ABOUT KATY LEE

 #1 Publishers Weekly best-selling author Katy Lee has penned over forty novels full of character-driven intrigue, romance and inspiration. She is a multi-award nominee for both the RITA® Award and Daphne du Maurier Award for her excellence in mystery and suspense. Katy lives in Utah's beautiful, rugged mountains where she is a special education teacher and runs a literary non-profit called Story Haven Writers to help people write their stories. Keep up with Katy and her latest news, including her monthly newsletter, "Novel ideas," at KatyLee-Books.com.

Interact with Katy Lee at:
Website: http://www.katyleebooks.com/

facebook.com/KatyLeewriter

instagram.com/katyleeauthor

bookbub.com/profile/katy-lee